DOWNSIZED

Caroline,
Don't let your vision be
downsized
and never give up!
Enjoy,
J. Wilson

outsource the entire purchasing and contract bidding department."

This was not what John wanted to hear. He tried to tune the whole thing out. He thought about running, but his legs felt like lead pipes and wouldn't have carried him far. He had to sit there, adjust himself in the hard chair, and accept his fate.

John felt Alan look at him, as if to be sure he was still with him while he finished the act. "You'll have to clear your desk and turn in your keys and badge immediately. Security is waiting for you outside the door. Good luck, John. I wish you the best. Here is an excellent letter of recommendation to help with your next position."

John could see that Alan's exhaustion was overwhelming him, the result of going through the same bleak dialogue with each member of the department he had groomed into a well-oiled machine. Since Alan was a middle manager, he had no windows in his office. John scanned the room, looking for something to focus on—the rim of the metal wastebasket, the plastic protective mat under Alan's chair. Even Alan's computer screen offered little diversion from the scene.

Unsure of what else to do, John stood, held out his hand, and with his usual obedience, accepted the envelope Alan handed him. Feeling shaky, he walked to the door. "Thanks" was all he could manage. John looked over his shoulder and saw someone follow him as he shuffled back to his desk. An empty copy paper box had appeared on his desk as if by magic. John mumbled out loud, "I guess this is for my stuff."

He managed to put the picture of his mother and another of him with Karen, his wife, in the box along with a few other mementos. John endured the regulation uniformed security officer hovering over him and chiding, "Come on, man. We don't have all day. Get that stuff in the box. No dillydallying."

Chapter **ONE**

ALAN, THE DEPARTMENT head, leaned against the door-jamb of his office, arms wrapped tightly around him. His head ached. He rubbed his eyes in frustration and walked toward John, his prize employee. "John, I need you to come into my office."

John paled. He saw his coworkers quickly turn their heads back to work, glad that Alan hadn't called their name. He heard a group of women gathered at the bank of file cabinets, "Him? This must be bad." Still standing, he grabbed his suit jacket from the back of his chair, put it on, buttoned it closed, and smoothed it to perfection out of habit. The bright over-head fluorescent lights exposed his brown, well-trimmed hair, which was flawlessly in place, as his dark, intense eyes stared straight ahead. He made his way to Alan's office; it seemed a mile away.

John sat in the chair across from Alan's metal, institutional, managerial-sized desk and gripped its arms to make sure he wouldn't slip to the floor.

Alan started, "John, I want you to know this is possibly the hardest thing I've ever had to do. Management has decided to

John's story isn't about one particular person. It really belongs to thousands of really bright people who have worked hard and dedicated their lives to their careers. *The Detroit News* did a series of articles about how different people were dealing with lay-offs and what they were doing with their severance packages. As I progressed through John's story every day for most of 2007, I scanned the papers for more articles about the Detroit economy and for the stories of individual sojourns through the murky jungle of redefining oneself. This was my research—the lives of my neighbors. *Downsized* is my reaction to these various stories.

My life has been changing from stay-home-mom to...something else. My youngest daughter is about to leave home; the fact is that I too am being downsized from my career of the past twenty years. I have experienced the process of realigning my life and priorities; the story I was given for John Sheppard applies to me. I have come to appreciate the importance of keeping faith first when making the exciting journey through the various phases of life!

I continue to read the papers every morning, but now this exercise is filled with a different expectation. I am looking for stories that reflect how faith is working in our community and in the lives of my neighbors.

Introduction

I START EACH DAY reading the newspapers from cover to cover. Not just one paper; I read both Detroit papers, you know, in case I miss something. Up until 2006, I wasn't really looking for anything in particular. I would frequently lift a word of prayer for various victims of stories or perhaps a word of praise for the infrequent good news one might find there. Sometimes I might actually know the person in the story. Basically, I'm just a news junky.

The news around the Detroit area and pretty much all of Michigan has been pretty grim. We seem to be spiraling downward, scratching and clawing for a reprieve. When I came across the story in the Local Section of *The Detroit Free Press* about a man who needed rescue from the back of a garbage truck, a man with a cell phone, but no job, who wasn't drunk or homeless, my imagination went crazy. The newspapers have been filled for months with stories about job lay-offs in the automotive industry, a theme dominating the lives of everyone in southeastern Michigan. I decided that these stories belonged together.

I especially need to thank my parents, Bob and Shirley Warkentien, for loving and believing in me for so many years and for your enthusiasm of my first writing efforts.

The belief in my abilities of my entire family made it impossible for me to let this effort flounder or even to quit.

I would also like to thank Miranda Burnett for her editing and the professional direction she gave my work. We sweated through many rewrites to ready the manuscript for presentation to a publisher, and I appreciate your diligence and patience. Along with Miranda's efforts was the support of the Wednesday Writers, my writing group who listened and critiqued much of the manuscript, getting it ready for publication.

The product before you is a tribute to the wonderful staff at Creation House. From Sue Teubner, acquisitions editor, to Virginia Maxwell, the production manager, to Atalie Anderson, the marketing coordinator, everyone has been incredibly helpful and incredibly creative. It has been a thrill to me to work with such talented individuals.

Finally, I need to acknowledge my Lord, Jesus Christ, who blessed me with this story at just the right time in my life. To Him I give the glory, honor, and praise for this humble effort.

Acknowledgments

I WANT TO TAKE this opportunity to thank several people for their help with this project. It goes without saying, that without their assistance, this work could not have been completed.

First, I need to acknowledge and thank Scott, my husband of almost twenty-eight years, who, from the day we were assigned to be debate partners in high school, has never allowed me to accept a mediocre effort from myself. You have modeled and preached a student's mentality which has enriched my life and which I have not been able to ignore. You have always encouraged me to take whatever I was doing to the next level and specifically to move from a simple manic reader to a writer, to a published author.

Second, I need to acknowledge and thank my two wonderful daughters, Emily and Elle. I have watched each of you set goals, take risks, and work hard to achieve your dreams. Your father and I love supporting your efforts. It has been gratifying to receive the reciprocal support from you.

DEDICATED TO:

Scott, Emily, and Elle
For your love, support, and encouragement.
Always striving for your best, living your dreams,
And serving the Lord with your every effort!

DOWNSIZED by Jill Wilkinson
Published by Creation House
A Strang Company
600 Rinehart Road
Lake Mary, Florida 32746
www.creationhouse.com

Unless otherwise noted, all Scripture quotations are from the New King James Version of the Bible. Copyright © 1979, 1980, 1982 by Thomas Nelson, Inc., publishers. Used by permission.

Design Director: Bill Johnson
Cover design by Justin Evans

Library of Congress Control Number: 2008936176
International Standard Book Number: 978-1-59979-481-5

First Edition

08 09 10 11 12 — 9 8 7 6 5 4 3 2 1
Printed in the United States of America

DOWNSIZED

JILL WILKINSON

CREATION HOUSE
A STRANG COMPANY

John turned his head so the obnoxious officer had to look him in the eye. "So who does the Rolodex belong to? Me or Ford?" He looked at the expressionless face as he waited for an answer. "Well, does it go in the box or not?" The security officer couldn't have cared less; he nodded to the box.

"Outsourcing? Purchasing? Ford Motor Company, one of the largest auto companies in the world, isn't going to have a purchasing department?" John rolled this around in his brain. Security nudged his elbow. "Keep going," he demanded. Soon the desk was emptied of all reminders of John Sheppard or the hours of work he completed there.

He reached into his pockets to pull out his keys and badge. He stared at the key chain, fingering each key and thinking, "No more office key?" He surrendered the office key and stared at the remaining keys, wondering how long they would get to stay.

Noticing the few coworkers left glaring at Alan's office to see who would receive the guillotine next, John picked up the box containing the remnants of his career, carelessly slipped on his new navy cashmere overcoat, left the office, and went to the elevator without saying anything. The security guard escorted him down the elevator and out the front door making sure there were no detours.

John felt the cold November wind blow right through him. He looked back at the door, the same door he walked through every morning with so much hope and excitement for the past nine-plus years. He shook his head and trudged across the parking lot to his 2007 blue Ford Escape.

"There it is," he thought, "the smell of exhaust from the freeway and factories; it's always made me think of productivity and financial security, but today it's mixed with the smell of decay from the dying leaves of fall, death."

In a daze, he stuck the box on the passenger seat next to him and plopped into the driver's seat. He went through the ritual of putting his key in the ignition, reaching for the seatbelt, pulling it across his chest, and finally clicking it into place. So many steps; they took so much effort. The car started and he put it into gear. That was it. All he could think of now was the dilemma—Where was he going to go? Where do you go when you've just lost your job? As if in a trance, he drove to the building across the street, where management was housed. He pulled into a parking space facing the building, turned off his car, and sat. The scene was like watching an old black-and-white movie on reel-to-reel film with no sound. It was kind of haunting.

He dragged the box toward him and processed its contents. He looked at his diplomas. "I've kept these in my bottom drawer for a year now, waiting for my promotion and a chance to hang them on the wall of an office." He looked at the windows of the infamous Glass House and thought, "Now I'll never be a part of that society," which had been his dream since childhood.

"Maybe I should call someone. Who? I don't want to tell this to anyone, not even Karen. It's too...I don't know. It's just not me." He continued to sit there, silently, brooding for hours.

People started exiting the building and hurrying out through the parking lot, the wind swirling and blowing their coats around their bodies. John began to feel conspicuous. Seeing that he was drawing unwanted attention, he decided, "I've got to get out of here."

He drove toward home, hardly noticing the changing scenery until the road came to a dead end. "Another decision," John lamented. "I can't concentrate. I just can't go home right now." He sat at a green light like a dummy trying to figure out what to do. The drivers behind him began honking. Exasperated with the whole thing and getting angrier by the minute, he yanked the steering wheel hard to the left, almost tipping his Escape as he recklessly turned and drove away from home, his neighborhood, and everything familiar.

After several miles, several traffic lights, and many twists and turns in the road, he spied another expressway ramp and drove down it. Heading to where? He didn't know and didn't care. Driving seemed to be the only thing that made sense right now. He needed to run away.

This trek allowed his brain to disengage from the world, but thoughts of fear and doubt assaulted his mind like missiles. "We've put some money into savings, not a whole lot. I wonder how long it will last? We sure can't afford the lifestyle we've had. God, we just started to enjoy ourselves a little, too, feeling like we could buy a few of the things we'd been putting off. We don't have any school debt, thanks to Ford. At least they let me finish my MBA before throwing me to the wolves. I'll bet that won't do me any good. I'll probably be overqualified now, too expensive."

The economy of the entire Detroit area was so awful; there was reason for the panic. The barrage of thoughts continued: "How long can we make it on just Karen's salary? Could we lose our house? If we need to sell, who'd buy it? No one's buying." Many people were losing their homes, unable to make the payments.

"Up until today, it was always other people, not us. God, we've worked so hard, played by the rules, did the corporate dance. What good was it?" he yelled into the empty vehicle and banged the steering wheel with his fist.

John couldn't think of another time in his life when he felt such lack of control. His head was spinning. He couldn't breathe. He loosened his tie, leaving it askew, and unfastened the top button of his shirt. Beads of sweat gathered on his brow. Somehow, he drove on.

What was Karen going to say? He worried about her reaction. Karen was ambitious, driven. What if they had to relocate in order for him to get another job and she didn't want to move? Why would she ever agree to leave her job? This was going to be disastrous. He could just see it. "We've been together forever, known each other through high school, college, career, and grad school. But that probably won't be enough to keep her from walking away. She'd never allow herself to be dragged down by me." John was really feeling sorry for himself, sure that he'd lost everything important in his life.

Looking out the window, he wondered where he was. Somehow he'd exited the expressway and wandered into a bad neighborhood, one he hadn't seen before. "How long have I been driving?" He looked at the clock on the dash and saw that it was already six o'clock at night. "I really don't like being lost." Hysteria rose within him and John started to take turns at random corners until he saw a street he thought he recognized. He wanted to go home, now, desperately.

The grayness of the day was turning to night; the blackness was unnerving. John absorbed the blight of the area, a scene he'd never experienced before.

The windows on many of the houses were boarded over, burned out, and never torn down or repaired. Despite their unsafe appearance, it looked like people still lived in them. The rest of the houses were abandoned, most likely used for drugs and prostitution. Trash, old tires, and discarded play structures filled the yards. Newspapers and fast-food wrappings were everywhere, gathered along the rusted and broken fences where the wind stacked them as if to build a wall to hide the despair beyond. The neighborhood was spotted with vacant lots, their brown grass overgrown and littered similar to the rest of the area.

There were a few strip malls that housed cash advance stores, party stores, little Chaldean groceries, and Church's Fried Chicken. Some of the stores were either vacant or closed; they were so dirty it was hard to tell. Drawn across the doorways were gates, rusty and falling off their hinges, while flashing neon lights on signs spelled out their names, drawing attention to the selection of burned out light bulbs.

There were bars everywhere: bars covering the windows and doors and bars to hide and drink away your sorrows and disappointments. Going into a bar didn't feel like an option for him; someone might ask him why he was there.

John kept driving, feeling a kinship with the street people. "They look so hollow," he mused as they watched him. He stared back at them like foreigners, aliens.

He slowly passed Saving Faith Baptist Church. The redbrick building looked slightly better than the community it served. "There's no way I'm going into a church; not now, not here or not anywhere. I don't want to talk to strangers—especially not God, not after the way He's treated me." His anger seethed as he thought about the difficulties of his life, now and those in his childhood.

John kept driving until his car slowed. Something was wrong. It didn't matter how hard he jammed the accelerator into the floor. "That's just great!" John slammed his fist again. "I'm out of gas." He was disgusted and sat at the side of the road with his head resting on the steering wheel. He let the tears come for the first time all day. John rarely cried, but today he felt raw, torn—and worthless. The tears turned to gasping sobs.

"Karen, why didn't I listen to you? I've made a mess of everything," he bellowed into the empty car. Still unsure what to do, where to go, or what was next, he reminded himself that he needed to think.

"Well, OK, first things first; I have to get gas." He started walking. It wasn't but a few houses later when he saw them—an intimidating bunch of men, maybe boys. They were approaching him and then suddenly spread out. They fit this neighborhood, large, hulking figures with baggy pants, waistbands across their butts hanging by what he didn't know, with crotches at their knees, probably hiding some kind of weapon or something. They wore huge dark, hooded sweatshirts, masking their identities.

Their postures indicated arrogance. This was their space and they ruled.

"Hey, man, check it out," said one.

"Well, whatta we got here?" said another.

"Yo dude, whatcha doin'? Who you lookin' at?" still another said as he bent into him and snarled.

They circled him, closing in, eliminating escape. They never stood still, always moving and weaving as if performing a dance, always keeping their eyes on John, mocking and tormenting him, waiting for the perfect moment to pounce.

"Um, I, I don't know." John held his hands out in front of him either to stop them from coming too close or to show them he meant no harm. The anxious sweat beaded his face and his heart felt like it was going to jump out of his chest any minute. He was shaking and his eyes were flicking from one thug to another trying to focus with no success. Feeling anger, fear, and desperation, he wasn't sure what was going to happen.

They laughed, taunting him. "Sucker."

John saw the weapons. Were they guns or knives? The thugs were all armed and threatened him.

John felt a warm wetness on his leg. How humiliating! He'd wet his pants.

The largest of them shouted at John, "Give me your keys and wallet or you're dead!"

John had no fight left in him; he desperately looked around for help, but there was none in sight. Powerless, he fumbled around in his pocket while they were all yelling and laughing at him, finally locating the keys. He surrendered the keys and wallet, dropping them on the pavement with little resistance.

The smallest of the gang scrambled to scoop up the goods; they all ran back in the direction of John's abandoned car.

"At least," John thought, "they aren't going to get far with my car on empty." But then he realized they weren't going to get far, which meant they'd be back for him. He knew he had to move quickly before they returned, angry and demanding vengeance. He needed a place to hide—a safe place—now.

Then he saw them behind the half-deserted strip mall—yes, the Dumpsters. There were three of them. He could hide back there. He raced behind the stores looking over his shoulder, constantly making certain his enemies weren't close behind. "This place is horrible," John looked around. "Ugh, everything is so disgusting; this filth is unimaginable."

John started to shake. Nervous tension overtook him again. He rubbed his face with both hands. "Man, I was afraid when I was just lost, but now I'm going to get beaten to death. Oh God." He tried to hide behind the Dumpsters, but there was still too much visibility from the parking lot lights. "I don't have any option."

Bucking it up, he began to climb into the Dumpster. John grabbed the top edge of the Dumpster and tried to pull himself up, but the angle was wrong and he couldn't make it. He fell back, landing with a groan in a puddle and splashing the repulsive combination of stagnant water, urine, and alcohol all over him. He jumped up, quickly shaking himself off and scanned the area. He found some large boxes and metal drums and dragged them to the base of the dumpster on the side away from the street. He climbed on top of the stack and managed to lift his left leg, hampered by his wet, sticky pants over the edge. Using all the strength he could muster, he pulled himself the rest of the way up using his hands, chin, and arms. Down he went inside the Dumpster and collapsed on a pile of garbage.

As John crouched down, trying to conceal himself from the street, he reached into his pocket and turned off his cell phone so that it wouldn't give him away.

The stench of the Dumpster, a rancid combination of rotten meat, spoiled vegetables, and stale alcohol, was overwhelming. Death and pestilence were so pervasive in this part of the city that they became a part of John in the Dumpster. John gagged and choked back the bile. He closed his eyes, holding his breath as long as he could.

"Oh God, when will I be safe? At least no one's going to look for me here. The real question, though, is, who would want me where I am now?" As he closed his eyes, his heavy brows relaxed. His lips, which had been pursed together in a perpetual grimace all day, finally released. All the muscles in his face ached from the day's tension. Every bone in John's body screamed against the pain and horror he felt, then slowly, his body crumpled, he rested on top of the trash and passed out.

Chapter TWO

FINISHED WITH HER work for the day as a financial analyst at Cargill Electronics, Karen prepared to go home. She decided to call John and let him know she was in charge of dinner.

She put some papers to review that evening into her briefcase and thought, "I'm so lucky to have John. He's really been there for me, especially this past month while I've been working day and night on this contract. I know Brad is going to be pleased; the negotiations are right on track." Not only was Brad her boss of almost ten years, but he was also her friend and mentor.

Karen sat at the desk in her cubicle for a couple of minutes, thinking how fortunate she was to have a job that she loved so much. She brushed her long, thick black hair away from her face and knotted it at the base of her neck. She recrossed her long legs under the desk and wiggled her toes in her designer pumps, a splurge she knew was extravagant—but which she never regretted. She called them her power shoes, and felt like a force to be dealt with when she wore her Jimmy Choos. After brushing the skirt of her black, sleek, Tory Burch suit she thought, "I couldn't have put this deal together without John. He's been my rock."

Karen continued her happy reverie. "Yes, John's been there for me, every night for the last month, no matter how tired he might have been. He's been great, supported me as I sweated out the rewrites and listened as I practiced every element of this proposal. He contributed some of the best ideas, too. If he hadn't listened to me and given me feedback, there is no way I could have negotiated with such cool confidence as effectively. I love it. Our nightly work sessions empower me."

Karen thought back to high school. "Boy, he was so good looking: tall, athletic, brilliant, and directed." They were a good-looking couple. Mr. Clark, the debate coach, had seen it when he assigned them to be partners. They'd been together ever since.

Karen picked up the receiver and called John's office number. She was surprised when the call forwarded to some other line with a strange voice answering.

"Hi, this is Karen Sheppard, I'm calling for John Sheppard."

The person on the other end typed the name in her computer, "I'm sorry, I don't have anyone by that name in my computer."

"What? You probably just misspelled it." Karen gave her the proper spelling and the typing began again.

"I'm sorry, nothing is coming up on my screen."

Karen thought, "This is just like directory assistance; some-times computers screw things up more than they help."

Karen continued, "May I please speak to your supervisor? I need to reach my husband and I know he works there."

"No problem, ma'am. Please hold."

After a moment's delay another voice came on the line. "Communications. May I help you?"

"Yes, thank you. I'm trying to reach my husband, John Shep-pard, and the operator was unable to connect me to his phone. Can you help me, please?"

She typed in the name, and when nothing came up she checked the list of changes human resources sent down that day. Turning to the page with the *S*'s, she spotted it immediately. She sure wasn't paid enough to tell this woman that her husband had been laid off. This kind of thing was happening all too often. She responded, "I'm sorry, but the operator was correct. Your husband is not on the roster."

"What happened?"

"I don't know any details, Mrs. Sheppard. I'm just the night supervisor in communications."

"Well, may I speak to someone in his department please?" Karen was agitated, but she was more concerned than anything. This wasn't right!

"I'm sorry, Mrs. Sheppard, but there isn't anyone here right now. It is after hours." From her paperwork, she knew that the whole department had been eliminated, but again, she wasn't about to be the one to tell this woman.

"OK, fine. Thanks anyway." Karen hung up, staring for a few minutes while trying to process the situation.

She tapped her fingers on her desk protector wondering why he hadn't called her. "He must already be home," she thought as she dialed their home number. She needed to be sure he was all right. No answer. She called his cell phone. No answer. Where was he? Now she was really worried. She grabbed her briefcase, keys, and coat, then ran for the door.

Karen got to her Mustang GT, threw her stuff in the back seat, jumped in, and put her seatbelt on while screeching out of the parking lot. She raced home, arriving in seven minutes, record time. John's Ford Escape was not in the driveway. She tried his cell phone again. Still no answer.

Karen ran into the house and immediately checked the answering machine; only one message played, and she heard her own voice earnestly calling for John to pick up the phone and then after no reply, to call her at once. She dumped her stuff on the floor, looked around the redbrick colonial house they'd bought four years ago, and tried to make sense of the situation.

It didn't look like he'd been home all day; nothing had been disturbed. "Where is he? He hasn't called me; maybe he called his mom." Karen quickly called her mother-in-law, Sharon. John was close to his mother since she'd been all he had for most of his life, so it wasn't unreasonable that he would have gone to his mom if he needed to talk, Karen rationalized.

"Hey Mom, have you heard from John today?" Karen started. Without waiting for an answer, she rushed on. "Do you know where he is?"

"Karen, what's wrong? You sound panicked. Is everything OK?"

"Mom, I don't know where John is. I called his office a little while ago, and it seems he doesn't work there anymore. I don't know what happened. He isn't home, and he isn't answering his cell. I was really hoping you'd heard from him." Karen was near tears. "What should we do?"

"I'll be right there, honey. Just hold on tight."

"No, Mom. What if he tries to call you at home? I think you should stay there, at least for a little while."

"OK, let's give him some time to contact one of us. Call me the second you hear anything."

It was seven o'clock. Karen had been waiting for one long hour and still hadn't heard a thing. "When is he going to call?" she wondered. Karen tried his cell about every ten minutes, to no avail. She kept pacing, wringing her hands and trying to figure out what to do and whom else she should contact. "John doesn't have that many close friends, no one he would have gone to instead of me." She changed into some more comfortable clothes, jeans and a long sleeve T-shirt. Her work clothes were too constricting with the panic she was experiencing.

At around ten o'clock, Karen called the police. "Hello, I'm Karen Sheppard, and I'd like to report my husband missing."

"How long has he been missing?"

"I don't know for sure. I spoke to his office and was told that he didn't work there anymore, but I haven't heard from him at all. I don't know where he is or if he's all right. I don't know anything." The panic in her voice gave way to her tears.

"Ma'am, until your husband has been missing for twenty-four hours, we can't do anything. I'm sure he's all right. You'll hear from him soon. Have you tried his friends or business associates?"

"I can't think of anyone John would have gone to. Something is wrong, and I need your help. Have there been any accidents? He might be hurt."

"Can you describe him? I'll check on your description." The dispatcher was trying to be helpful with the little she could do.

"Yes, he's six feet tall, dark hair, trimmed short. He weighs about 170 pounds and is in great shape, very athletic."

"What race?"

"White."

"I've checked my screens and nothing comes up fitting that description. If you want to be certain, though, you could call the area emergency rooms and other police stations directly."

"Thanks for your help," Karen said as she hung up, discouraged. She paced for a few more minutes and then began to call the emergency rooms, starting with those closest to the Ford offices.

"Hello, Oakwood Hospital Emergency Room. How can I help you?"

Karen wasn't sure what to ask. "Ah, yes, hello. My name is Karen Sheppard and I'm looking for my husband. I was wondering if he's there. His name is John Sheppard."

The emergency room clerk responded in an unemotional, robot-like voice, "Due to federal privacy laws, we are no longer allowed to disclose that kind of information."

"All I want to know is if my husband is injured and has been brought to your hospital. How difficult could this be?" Her voice betrayed the hysteria that was overtaking her.

The woman continued her practiced, emotionless reply: "I'm sorry, ma'am. I assume your husband is an adult, so we must respect his privacy."

"Are you saying my husband is there and you just can't tell me?" Karen questioned, impatient.

"No, I'm just saying we couldn't tell you if he were here."

"Can you tell me if you have anyone matching my husband's description?"

The desk attendant really did want to help Karen, even though her hands were tied with bureaucratic red tape. "I guess I could help you out to that extent. What does he look like?"

Karen repeated the detailed description of John.

"I'm sorry. No one has been brought in fitting that description."

Karen repeated this over and over again as she worked her way through each hospital and then each police station in the tri-county area. Some were more understanding than others, but no one had any answers for her. Karen just had to wait and hope

John would call home soon. She felt so helpless, unlike anything in her entire life. What could possibly be happening to John? This was completely out of character for him. Exhausted, she began to fear something terrible must have happened to him.

Chapter THREE

JOHN WAS AWAKENED by sudden, strange, inner-city, vehicle noises. The acrid stink that immediately assaulted his senses was worse than it had been a few hours earlier. He shuddered violently. His dirty clothes clung to him while his spent body ached from the cold and damp surroundings. He tried to wrap his overcoat more tightly around him as he moved his head slowly from side to side. "Oh God. Where am I?"

Consciousness began to flow into him like blood pulsing in his sleeping veins. It seemed he'd wedged himself into the corner of the Dumpster, lying on an acrid mixture of wet papers and boxes, glass bottles, and spoiled, discarded food. He smelled the stagnant water and alcohol and thrashed about, trying to stand up, but instead felt his body sink closer and closer to the bottom of the Dumpster.

"I've got to get out of here!" he cried. "But how?" The blackness was ominous; the lights in the parking lot were off. John couldn't even figure out which way was up. John guessed it had been hours since his encounter with the muggers.

His arms and legs flailed, causing more spoiled, stinky, discarded food; sticky, drippy bottles and cans; and used, gooey food wrappings to fall on him. With the little strength left in his body, he scratched and kicked, hoping to find some escape. He was desperate to grab hold of something to haul himself up. He couldn't reach the top edge of the Dumpster and nothing else held. Each attempt forced him backward, deeper in the heap of pungent debris.

By now his face, neck, and hair were smeared with a combination of the cold, stinky waste. It got into his nose and ears, even his mouth. John turned to his side, convulsed, and vomited the remnants of his last meal, which had probably been sixteen hours earlier.

John thought how easy it would be to simply let go, like a person trapped in an avalanche, overpowered by snow. He felt the same breath-stealing confinement, encased by the enormous strength of the snow or in John's drama, the garbage. But he couldn't let go. Something in his gut made him continue to fight. He couldn't quit.

The noise in the Dumpster caused by his panicky tantrum was joined by a thundering, gear-grinding, diesel-like sound. John heard it getting louder and louder. Something gigantic and menacing was coming at him. It sounded like a huge, powerful steam locomotive. His brain tried to comprehend what it was while the Dumpster shook as if it were in an earthquake; whatever it was had run right into it, and John was sure it was going to keep on going. His eyes opened wide with terror and fear stiffened his body. John screamed, out of his mind with panic, as the Dumpster rocked out of its place in the parking lot and started to lift in the air, with John in it.

"What's happening?" he cried. "Help, help, help!" John screamed at the top of his lungs until his throat was raw. "Help me! I'm here." He hit and kicked all sides of the Dumpster as he somersaulted up into the air, his muscles and joints yanked out of place by the force. The law of gravity kicked in, and he dropped back down again. He felt warm blood run down his arms and neck. His whole world literally turned upside down as he was flung into another metal cage with the rest of the trash. It began to move, and finally, John knew, he came to a rest in the belly of a garbage truck. "Oh, what now?" he thought aloud.

John felt around in the pocket of his jacket, and by some miracle his cell phone was still there. He pulled it out, discovered it was off, and jammed the buttons trying to turn on the power. "Come on, come on," he repeated. He was exasperated by the delay. "Don't take so long!" Another miracle. He heard the familiar chime of the phone turning on. "I can't believe I have service," he said, and dialed 911.

"Emergency, how can I help you? What is your location please?"

John yelled over the noise of the truck. "I don't know. I think I'm in the back of a garbage truck."

"Excuse me, sir. Is this a prank?" But the terror in his voice and the noise in the background told her he wasn't.

"No, please believe me." He smudged the tears from his face as he continued, "I got caught in a Dumpster and now I'm in a garbage truck. Help me please! You've got to send help."

The dispatcher responded to the desperation in his voice. Her training kicked in. "We'll get you help. Just try to stay calm. I'm connecting to the police now."

John was bouncing and jostling all over the place; he couldn't stand, and he couldn't lie still, either. The truck drove to its next stop. The truck's engine was so loud that at times he couldn't hear the dispatcher. He screamed into the phone, "Hello, hello? Are you there?" There was no response, not even a crackly, faint one. "Don't hang up. Don't leave me!" he wailed. He knew he'd lost the call. He felt around and discovered that the battery had fallen out of his phone. It was gone, and he couldn't call back. He couldn't help them find him. He was going to die in a garbage truck on the same day he lost his job. What an epitaph of his life. All the frustration of the day came out in a wild, shrieking, gut-wrenching, sobbing torrent of anger—"I deserve better than this!"

Meanwhile, the 911 dispatcher contacted the Oak Park Police through the Emergency Computer Link and transmitted the details of the emergency. She guessed the caller was in Oak Park from the signal on her computer telling her which cell tower was transmitting the call. When the call went dead unexpectedly, she took a deep breath; put her hands together, fingers intertwined; and squeezed to release the tension, sending up a prayer that help would get to him on time before the garbage truck compacted its load—and him along with it. It was all she could do at the moment.

The garbage truck made a couple more stops, and more refuse piled on top of John. It enveloped him, making it difficult to get any air and suffocating any hope John had of rescue. He wondered how long it would be until the truck needed to compact its load, which he knew would probably end his life. He ran his fingers around his head and could feel a large bump starting to form. There was something sticky where it hurt, probably blood, but it could be any of the viscid substances around him. He knew no one could hear him outside the truck.

When they stopped again, John banged on the sides of the truck violently as he had at the earlier stops, pounding, screaming, trying to get anyone's attention. For a second John thought he was imagining that he heard someone bang on the outside of the truck. Adrenalin flooded his body as he banged on the sides of the truck and screamed with a new vigor he didn't know he had. There the sound was again. There was definitely someone on the outside banging back. John felt a new surge of hope.

The police offers knew they'd found their guy. They quickly ran to the front of the truck and hit the door with their nightsticks, startling the poor garbage men to death.

The officer on the driver's side yelled at the men over the noise of the truck, "You've got a man in the back of your truck. Empty your load on the driveway, now!"

Confused, the garbage men did as they were told and heaved the lever on the floor of the truck's cab. The back of the garbage truck began to rise. As the truck's garbage bin reached it's tipping point, John, covered in debris and soaked in sweat, skidded down the floor of the bin as if he were on a well-greased slide. He landed with a thump on the driveway with all of the truck's night collections falling on top of him. John jumped to his feet, putting the maximum distance he could between himself and the horrible mess. Without noticing the small crowd of onlookers, he smiled from ear to ear. He was free. He may have wanted to hug the officers, but the stench kept the officers at bay. John cried with relief; he had suffered some cuts and scrapes on his hands and head, but he had received a second chance at life. He collapsed on the ground with no physical strength left to even hold him up. He had truly believed he was a goner.

"You know, man, that dispatcher saved your life," one of the police offers told him. "If I'd taken that call, I don't know if I'd have believed a guy was stuck in a garbage truck." He looked at his watch. "It took us only fifteen minutes to find and rescue you." Turning to his partner as the emergency crew prepared to take John to the hospital, the officer said, "This is one for the books."

It was one o'clock in the morning when the phone rang at the Sheppard's home, and Karen jumped, startled. She answered it on the first half-ring since she had been sitting with her hand on the receiver, a vigil she'd kept all night.

"Hello? Yes, this is Karen Sheppard." Even though she'd been waiting for the phone to ring, now that it did she was so nervous she could barely speak.

"Mrs. Sheppard, we have your husband, John, here at Providence Hospital."

"Oh, thank God. Is he all right?" She was almost afraid of the response.

"Yes, he appears to be fine. He needs to picked up, and please bring him a fresh set of clothes."

"What happened? Was he in an accident?"

"I'm sorry, Mrs. Sheppard, but you'll need to ask him what happened yourself."

"Thank you so much. I'll be there in ten minutes."

Karen quickly called Sharon. They would meet at the hospital.

As Karen drove to Providence, she prayed out loud with tears streaming down her face. "God, I know we've been strangers, but please help John. I can't imagine what I'm going to find, but it's got to be bad. I love him—help me to make sure he knows it."

By the time Karen reached the hospital, her mascara was smeared across her face and wisps of hair had fallen out of her ponytail. After pulling into a parking space close to the hospital entrance, she took a minute to pull herself together. She found a tissue in her purse and wiped the skin under her eyes. Checking herself out in the car mirror, she pulled out her ponytail, letting her hair fall loosely. She grabbed her purse and ran into the hospital to finally reunite with John.

After going through the burdensome rigmarole at the reception desk, Karen was shown to the curtained treatment room where John was waiting. Karen found John, showered, cuts cleaned and bandaged, wearing a pale blue hospital gown. "John, what happened to you? I've been scared out of my mind." She raced toward him, dropping her purse on a chair by the door.

He grabbed her and held her in his arms as tightly as he could. Sharon came into the area after Karen, and John reached for her as well. All three of them stood together hugging and sobbing. No one was rushing them, and it took quite a while for them to be able to let go. The fear of never having this moment together had been all too real.

Karen handed John the clean jeans and sweatshirt she brought. He changed quickly and was discharged from the hospital. As Karen led him out of the hospital, a nurse said, "Good luck to you."

Although the shower and clean clothes helped remove the stench of the night's activities, John still felt queasy and limp. He couldn't remove the images from his mind. Aware that he should have been relieved that he was safe, John nonetheless knew the real problems of his life were still there—he still had to tell his mother and Karen about losing his job. As the three of them headed to the parking lot, they all knew there was a lot to talk about.

Chapter **FOUR**

THE REALITY OF John's night of horror returned as the eerie orange glow of the parking lot lights shone against the stark blackness. In just twenty-four hours, their lives had been tipped upside down.

"My car—it's still somewhere in Oak Park."

"Well, do you have any idea where it is?" Karen asked.

John stood in front of her, slumped, exhausted, beat. "No." He hung his head. "When the garbage men were questioned, they had no clue. I think they were stunned I was hiding in a Dumpster at all."

John hadn't yet told Karen or his mother the details of his trauma. With each little disclosure, he could hear them catch a breath; he could see they had to work harder and harder to resist crying.

"I think I was on Lahser Road in Oak Park. One of the last things I remember clearly was seeing the road sign for Lahser before I ran out of gas. We'll need to stop for gas if we are going to get my car. Do you think we should do it tonight or wait until tomorrow?"

John didn't wait for an answer before continuing. "I should probably drive down there and get it now. I want to get this whole thing behind me tonight. I don't want to think about having to face it tomorrow. Do you have the second set of keys for the Escape?"

Karen didn't know how to respond. She wasn't sure how much more he could handle. She wasn't much better; her hands were clammy holding on to the strap of her purse, and her stomach was in knots. She was on the verge of hysterics, watching the vein in John's forehead throb. Driving around in rough neighborhoods in the middle of the night had to be a bad idea. She wanted to save her husband from reliving whatever it was he'd experienced and whatever provoked him to climb into that Dumpster in the first place. Karen checked her key chain. "I do have the keys, but...I don't know, honey. I think maybe we should go tomorrow when you've had some rest."

John still wasn't listening. He stared into space and repeated himself, "We'll have to get some gas for it. That's why I had to abandon the car."

"John, why didn't you call me for help?" This was the question that had been on her mind for hours, since she tried to call John at work.

John turned and looked toward her, but with a glassy stare. "I don't know. I couldn't talk to anyone, I guess." At least this time Karen felt John respond to her. Karen took charge of the situation.

"OK then, Mom, will you go back to our house and fix some soup or something? John, if you think it's important to get your car now, I'll take you." She looked at Sharon, begging patience. "We'll call you in a little bit and let you know what's going on."

Sharon nodded; she walked to her car alone. Standing together, John and Karen watched her until she was safely in her car.

Karen turned to John and took hold of his hand tenderly and firmly as she led him to her car in the lot. "Here we go."

They rode in silence as they left the hospital and drove toward Oak Park. The streetlights flashed a rude, regular pattern of light into the car as they drove down the street. Karen could tell that John was in another world. She lapsed into a world of her own as well. "I want to know what happened to him," she thought. "No, I *need* to know. How am I supposed to help him if I don't know what's going on in his head?"

Finally, she broke their silence. "John, I'm sorry that I've been so self-absorbed lately. I didn't have any idea what you were going through at work." More silence followed.

As the car continued toward Oak Park, John studied his wife. "She is so beautiful with her dark brown hair falling to her shoulders and those skinny jeans and T-shirt under her winter jacket," he noticed. "Karen's a take-charge person, but this one is out of her league. Our relationship is built on the fact that we are equals: equally driven, equally workaholic, equally ambitious. We understand each other; we don't judge when one career comes before the other. We're both too busy to even notice. There's no doubt about it; Karen's a winner. She picked the best company to jump-start her career. She attacks negotiations, loves the battle. She's a pro."

As he considered his own choices, the thoughts became uglier and more desperate. "I'm no winner. Look at me; I'm going nowhere. I picked a large corporate ship for my career, one that would be difficult to fall off. But I managed to fall anyway. Now, I have nothing, and I have to watch Karen as she heads off to work each morning. How is she going to deal with living with someone who has no place to go every morning?" John struggled to imagine their future together. How could he express what he was feeling or explain what happened? He looked at Karen; she'd always been his best friend, but he felt so distant from her.

"Karen, I don't know what to say. I can't find the words. I've never felt so lost. Right now, I don't even recognize myself. I've always had a job, always! It feels like I've lost more than just a job. It feels like I've lost everything."

She gulped back a sob. Fighting the urge, every fiber of her being wanted to rush in and fix him. "Honey, you are one of the most talented people I've ever met. You're hard working, reliable, and creative. You're going to be all right. We'll pull out of this."

Karen wasn't going to let him wallow. That was exactly what he'd been doing for the last several hours and it nearly cost him his life. "Karen, do you really believe that?" he asked.

"Well," she paused, trying to find just the right words, the words that would convince him that she believed in him. "You know I don't say things just to make you feel better. Yes, I believe it. I know you. I'll put my money on you any day and especially today."

They drove up and down the streets of Oak Park and around Lahser Road looking for his car. It was dark, quiet, and the wetness of the oily roads shimmered from the headlights. The desolation of the neighborhood was not nearly as obvious as it was in the light of day.

As he stared out the window, John thought, "I was lucky I wasn't in an accident, driving that many hours without paying attention. How stupid of me. I could have killed myself or other people. This isn't like me. I'm usually so careful to follow all the rules. I pride myself on being a smart, sensible person. I sure proved that wrong today." He shook his head. The vein on his forehead throbbed visibly.

Both John and Karen had known people who had been laid off. The routine was to disappear from view for a while, reappearing when they got their act together and were ready for public exposure. However, Karen never had firsthand experience with anyone so shaken. She thought about how it was easier to forget about the person who was laid off and hurting when he or she wasn't right in front of you. Now, she could look over and see its effect on someone she loved. She could observe for the first time how his identity and value had been eliminated. Karen believed John would come out all right; he would be valuable to another company. But for the time being, she saw he was in shock and doubted his future.

John brought her out of her thoughts by pointing to his Ford Escape across the street; at least he thought it was his. "Apparently since they couldn't start my car and couldn't steal it—they decided I couldn't have it either," he said. The Escape was barely recognizable. All the windows were smashed; the headlights and taillights were destroyed, and the grill was kicked in. They must have taken something large and heavy to the doors, hood, and trunk. It was hard to imagine baseball bats causing that much damage. The tires were slashed as well. Karen and John were dumfounded at the anger the muggers had directed at the Escape. Karen picked up her cell phone and called the police. She was able to give them good directions to where they were located.

As they waited for the police to arrive, the couple walked over to the SUV to look around—and then it hit him. The trash strewn around the vehicle was the stuff that had been in the box in the front seat. Both Karen and John felt sick at the sight of what had been pieces of John's career. Broken silver frames holding pictures of John's mother and Karen lay in the gutter next to framed diplomas and certificates with the carelessness of someone with no idea of what work and sacrifice went into acquiring them. John's Rolodex, containing the contact information for all of his friends and business acquaintances, lay on the curb covered in mud. There under the car, just barely visible was the envelope Alan gave him with his severance information. The sight of such destruction and recklessness was almost too much to handle. The destruction could very well have included John's body if those thugs had found him again. This reality was not wasted on them as Karen and John leaned on each other, spent and disgusted, and waited for the police to come.

John looked at Karen, "I lost my job! Our whole department was downsized."

"I know, honey. I called your office at the end of the day, and the switchboard operator told me they didn't have a John Sheppard working there. I thought it was some sort of mistake, but I guess it's real."

Karen choked back the tears, wiping them away before John would notice. Would the fear and frustration of this day ever end? She wanted to get John back home, safe and sound, so badly, but she knew deep in her heart that "safe and sound" was a long way off.

Turning to John, she said, "I love you so much. I can't stand how close I came to losing you tonight. We need to stick together. We have to be able to talk. I know you've been through something awful tonight. I was so scared, but not knowing if you were dead or alive was the worst. I need you to keep me in the loop. I can't be there for you unless I know what's going on." She dug her fingers into his shirt, clinging for dear life.

The lights got their attention as the police cruiser pulled up behind them. They were different officers than those who'd rescued John, but apparently "the saga of the Dumpster man" had made its way through the force already.

"Well, Mr. Sheppard, you've had quite a night!"

John looked at the officer, hoping to avoid conversation about the whole ordeal, "Yes, sir."

"Can you describe the men who attacked you?"

"Honestly, I didn't really see anything to help you. They all wore baggy pants that hung down and huge, dark sweatshirts. Their faces were hidden, so I can't get very specific for you. They were various sizes, but mostly I'd say in the range of six feet tall with a big build. As you can see, they were mad when they found out there was no gas in my car."

"How many of them were there?"

"I didn't take the time to count, but just guessing, I'd say, probably seven or eight."

"What did they say?"

"They just harassed me and demanded my keys and wallet."

"Did they have weapons?"

"Yes, I think they all had some kind of weapon, maybe knives, but some may have had guns. I saw the flash of metal and didn't put up any fight. When they got what they wanted, they just ran off."

"You're pretty lucky. Usually, they like to inflict some pain and injury even when they get what they want. Approximately what time did this happen?"

"The last time I looked at the dashboard clock, it was six, so I'd say between six and seven."

The police took pictures of the Escape and made arrangements to have his car towed. John would need to call the insurance agent and take care of getting his car fixed in the morning.

John and Karen packed his belongings back into the paper box and headed for home. They were completely exhausted and hungry. They arrived home at two o'clock in the morning and found Sharon curled up on the beige corduroy couch in the living room.

"Thank God you're home. I couldn't leave until I knew you were OK," she said as she stood to tuck her blouse into her rumpled grey pants. "Did you find your car? Is everything OK?" she asked as she looked from John to Karen and back trying to figure out what happened.

Chapter FIVE

THEY WERE SITTING at the kitchen table trying to relax as Sharon dished tomato soup into large white ceramic soup bowls, took the grilled cheese sandwiches from the oven, and placed them on a dinner plate. She also poured each of them a glass of wine. "I know wine at this hour and with this food is a little strange, but it might help you relax and hopefully help you sleep," she said sweetly. She couldn't help but joke with John, "Since you've had a nap, you probably aren't as tired as the rest of us."

A little levity was her way of easing tough situations. There'd been enough of them in her life all ready. At sixty, Sharon was the kind of mother who always put everyone else ahead of herself. Her family and friends were her priority. All her energy was invested in those around her, whether a casual acquaintance or her only son. She didn't care much about fashion. Her clothes were out of date and she still wore her salt-and-pepper hair in tight pin curls. A casual observer might have described her as frumpy, but Sharon Sheppard captivated everyone with her sparkling blue eyes and her disarmingly warm smile. In all venues of her life, she was well loved.

"It's been almost thirty years since I lost your father, the lowest point of my life. You sure took me back there tonight, son."

"Yeah, I know, Mom. I'm sorry," John replied. He looked at his mother as she gave him that little wink, the one she always pulled out when the chips were down to let him know they would be all right. It still helped. Despite all of life's struggles, here they were—and they were in one piece. They were safe.

John kept his gaze at the table. "Why don't we all get some sleep and talk tomorrow?" He didn't want to spend the night rehashing the mess of the day with either of them. He wanted time alone. He wasn't through brooding. He wasn't through feeling sorry for himself, and this would be difficult with his two cheerleaders hanging around.

Karen said to Sharon, "Mom, why don't you stay in the spare room? I'd feel a lot better if you didn't drive home alone in the middle of the night."

Sharon hesitated, "Honey, that's very generous, but I think you two need your privacy in the morning. I should get out of here now and give you your space."

Karen wasn't about to give in, "No, Mom. We're family, and I don't want you driving in the middle of the night." She almost added that they'd had enough close calls for one day. Pointing to the bedroom, Karen looked at Sharon lovingly and continued, "Make yourself at home; I'll get you something to wear to bed."

Sharon nodded and went into the bedroom, closing the door behind her.

John was still sitting at the table, playing with a pile of salt that had spilled. He wasn't making any moves toward the bedroom. Karen stood looking at him after she gave Sharon a flannel nightgown. She knew his ego was badly bruised, but she knew that he possessed an inner strength, though not too visible now, that would help him through the crisis.

Karen walked over to John and kissed his forehead. "I'm going to bed now. If you need or want anything, please come and get me. I love you, John. I'm here for you." She turned and slowly walked from the room. She looked back at him over her shoulder. His position hadn't changed, so she continued on to the bedroom.

As she brushed her teeth, she stared into the medicine cabinet mirror and prayed silently for strength. It was so hard to know what to do.

Karen thought, "John is the same person I met and fell in love with in high school. We waited for our college acceptance letters and our job offers together. We have known tense times before. I think John has always worried about being good enough. He assumed he wouldn't get into the best school or get the great job. But that was a different kind of fear. That was in his head; this one is backed up with someone on the outside saying, 'We don't want you anymore. You're not valuable to us.' How do you argue that away? How can I help him now?" She shook her head, walked back to the bedroom, and changed her clothes. Slipping under the covers, she lay on the cool sheets staring at the ceiling. "I need to be here for him, but in the way that he needs me, not how I need to be needed." Karen fell asleep trying to figure this out.

Sharon quickly changed into the warm nightgown and sat on the bed. She thought about the little boy she raised alone since he was one year old. They had lived close to the Air Force base. Her husband, John Sr., had been part of a unit that was deployed overseas for six months of a one-year stint. Her mind returned to the day Air Force officers knocked at her door to tell her John had been killed in Lebanon. When she collapsed, they picked her up and carried her to the couch. Life was never the same.

"I know the fear John is experiencing," she thought. "I have felt my future snuffed out in an instant, that sudden desperate need to claw for air, for a reprieve. I prayed daily he would never have to experience it, but it was in the blackness that I found Jesus." She had her faith—the Lord carried her through the many storms and uncertainties she and little John had weathered together.

"All those years finding ways to pay for health care, rent, and food—I'll never forget the apprehension every time I opened the winter utility bills wondering where the money would come from. The Lord was always faithful, always standing close by me. Actually, it was amazing how things were taken care of; sometimes I'd be asked to help with a catering job with a friend or someone needed some babysitting and would call. The jobs were small, but they added up. We never had any reserves. I didn't even own a home until John's education was paid for, but we made it. The biggest downside of being a single parent is the constant fear of what would become of John if something happened to me.

"When John was older and showed so much academic promise, I knew I had to find a way to send him to college. Her husband had been smart, too; that's where John got his brains, but college was a pipe dream for him. That's why he joined the Air Force in the first place, to take advantage of the good old GI Bill. No, I worked to put John through college; I wasn't willing to lose my son the way I did John Sr."

Jesus had watched over them, guided, protected, and loved them through the years. Her prayers seemed endless to her at times, but that night Sharon dropped to her knees as she had many times before, folded her hands, and shut her eyes. "You must really get tired of hearing from me, Lord."

Chapter SIX

JOHN WAS STILL sitting at the kitchen table slouched in the chair, awake, and waiting for answers when Karen walked into the room to make coffee at seven the next morning. He never came to bed. In fact, he was in the same position she left him the night before—although it had been only a few hours. She went to hug him. He looked up at her with bloodshot eyes and a tear-streaked face. The confusion of the day before had not cleared.

Karen bent over and looked him straight in the eyes and said softly, "John, you'll figure this out. It is going to be OK, maybe even better than you would have done at Ford. We have each other; we have a lot that other people don't have. You'll see."

John cried again. Now that he'd begun crying, he couldn't seem to stop. Before yesterday, Karen had never seen John cry. She had seen him emotional, frantic, angry, and scared, but never teary. This wasn't normal, not for them.

Take-charge Karen came to life at those tears. "John, go take a shower. You'll feel better. I'll make breakfast and we'll make a plan for the day. I'm calling the office to tell them I won't be in today."

John got to his feet and obediently walked out of the room. Attempting normalcy, Karen turned to the refrigerator and took out eggs, bacon, bread, and butter. Then she walked over to the coffeemaker, threw coffee beans in the grinder, and pushed the button. Through the hum of the grinder she was focusing on what to say. It killed her to watch her husband suffer so. She started the coffee and reached down to pull out the frying pan. First, she placed strips of bacon into the pan and the bread went in the toaster. As the bacon cooked, she took a fork and whisked the eggs vigorously, working out her own frustration. Once the eggs were scrambled and the toast buttered, she put them on a simple white plate and put it on the table. The busyness gave her perspective, something tangible to accomplish. John and his mom both walked into the kitchen to the aroma of a hearty breakfast.

"Do you cook like this every morning? I might make this a regular stop!" Sharon exclaimed playfully.

Karen smiled at her mother-in-law, appreciating the levity. "Oh yeah, and I also make all my own bread and start my own pasta sauce, once I have scrubbed all the floors on my hands and knees before a full day at work." They both seemed to enjoy the joke and looked over at John to see if it had any effect on him.

John shuffled over to his seat at the table, trying not to engage with either of them. He picked up his coffee cup and held it mid-air for a moment before putting it back down on the table. He fiddled with the napkin and silverware with equal detachment.

Karen and Sharon joined him at the table with plates full of food. They looked at the enormous breakfast wondering if they could even eat. Exchanging glances, they tried desperately to figure out how to be the most helpful. They picked up their forks at the same time, pushing the food around and taking a few bites here and there. Small talk seemed inappropriate, leaving any communication difficult. John stared intently at his plate making sure he didn't make any eye contact with either his mom or wife. At last he ate; a mouth full of food made it easy to avoid conversation. Once finished, he pushed himself away from the table, folded his arms at his chest, and shifted his gaze out the window.

"Well, at least my résumé is up to date," he said blandly as the arbitrary thought suddenly hit him.

"That's a great start, honey. Didn't you have some head-hunters asking for it?" Karen asked a little too enthusiastically.

"I didn't know you were thinking of changing jobs," Sharon added.

"Mom, I haven't really been thinking of changing jobs. Headhunters always get the list of MBA graduates to contact for potential job opportunities. That's how they get paid. I wouldn't have considered it since Ford paid for my degree; I felt I owed them my loyalty to stay and work—a loyalty that I'm no longer obligated to," he trailed off. "I do have their names and numbers though. I guess I'll send them my résumé and let them know I'm available now."

"John, maybe you should talk to someone, a counselor maybe, before you contact headhunters, just to figure out the right approach. You want to make the best first impression possible, you know." Karen continued, "Who do you think would be good?"

"You're right—I don't want to come off too needy or desperate. Maybe I should call my advisor from grad school. We got along pretty well, and he had some great ideas when I was there." John wasn't sure that his old grad school advisor would even take his call; he hadn't spoken to him in almost a year. But some direction was better than nothing at this point. Anyway, it was a step closer to getting out of his predicament.

Sharon sat silently, wondering if there was anything she could add that would help. She rose and walked to the sink, rinsed the dishes, and put them in the dishwasher before asking, "Does anybody need more coffee?"

Both Karen and John looked up, startled out of their trance. The atmosphere in the kitchen was still awkward, but they managed a smile. Karen looked at her mother-in-law and said, "Keep it coming." Sharon put on a fresh pot.

John went into the garage and into Karen's car. He took out the box they'd retrieved from his car and brought it to the table. "We might as well face this," he said. He pulled out the envelope that Alan gave him, put it on the table, and stared at it. "What's that?" Karen asked.

Looking at the envelope in his hand as if it were a serpent he replied, "This? This is all I have left of my career; it's my severance package. I haven't looked at it yet." John answered. He shifted the envelope from one hand to another and put it back down on the table. "What am I afraid of? It seems silly to deny the reality of this situation. It's not like a college or job offer. I know what it says; I am unemployed. I need to find out what I am entitled to as a former employee of Ford Motor Company. I need to look in this envelope and see." John was mumbling to himself.

"Do you want me to look at it for you?" Karen asked, struggling to avoid taking over but wanting to help. He pushed the envelope toward her. She flipped it over and broke the seal. She drew out the papers and laid them on the table in a neat stack and began to read the cover letter. Sharon poured more coffee and John stared at her.

"They sure have this down to an art—no flowery language, pure and simple. Listen to this: 'We are sorry to have to inform you of the elimination of your position, effective immediately...' And it continues with, 'Please be advised that your years of service and level of achievement have entitled you to the following severance benefits.'"

Karen gave a cursory review of the benefits and even chuckled a little when she saw that they were relieving him of his prior education assistance commitment to remain with the company for four years and would not charge him for their expenditures for his MBA. She hadn't thought about the concept of Ford turning around and charging them for John's educational expenses. Guess that was a lucky break.

"Look, John, they're offering you financial advisory services for free; that's listed right after the acknowledgement of your MBA. There is something serendipitous about that, don't you think?"

John smiled stiffly before getting straight to the point. "OK, Karen, anything about money? That's what I want to know."

Karen looked on down the letter. "Oh, here it is. They are giving you six months' salary, payable in six monthly installments. Is that what you were expecting?"

"Actually, that's not bad. I've heard of people who haven't gotten any money," John replied. "Does it say anything about how much my health insurance will cost? I know I'll be paying for that."

"Oh, wow, that's going to cost $300 per month with a $500 deductible. I wonder what it would cost to add you to my plan at work. I'll call our human resource department and check it out. When do your current benefits expire?"

John stared back at the table as he answered, "I hope to be employed before eighteen months are up and that's my COBRA benefit period, I believe. But check out your plan. I think I'm good until the end of the month. I hope I was covered last night at the emergency room, or that was an expensive boondoggle. We sure don't need that bill. It would probably be a good idea to review our finances soon to make sure that we have enough to cover our living expenses."

Karen felt better suddenly because that was the kind of thinking that she was used to with John. "I think we should be in pretty good shape. You've been such a pragmatic planner, always thinking ahead with your game plan."

John was rarely caught unprepared because he believed in putting the work in up front. Over-preparing usually meant there were few surprises. Karen enjoyed the comfort that this provided them.

She reminded him, "Your constant planning and evaluation enabled us to buy this house when we found just the right deal. And don't forget that we were both able to return to school and complete our MBAs with no student debt because of this as well." She could tell that he wasn't receiving any reassurance. He needed to do something constructive.

"John, I know that you haven't slept all night, but why don't we go for a run? We haven't done that together for a long time; we could really use the stress release."

"I think you're right. I may not have slept, but I don't see myself lying down anytime soon. I'm too edgy. Yeah, a run sounds good. Mom, I think we're going to be OK for now. Are you going to hang out? I don't know what's on your plate for the day."

"OK, you guys, I'm going home. Things seem to be stable here for now. I'm supposed to be at church in a couple of hours for my Bible study, so I guess I'll get out of your way. Call me if you need anything. I love you both."

Sharon slipped out of the kitchen and into the bedroom to dress in the same clothes she had worn last night. A few minutes later she was in her own 2001 Ford Taurus and heading back home. She knew that they had some rough times ahead; things were pretty tough in the job market these days.

After she pulled into her driveway, she sat in her car for a few minutes and prayed, "Lord, I know you didn't bring John all this way to abandon him. He may have some hard lessons to learn in the days ahead but I know you have your hand on him. I trust you, Lord." Soon she was home and entered her small, cozy home feeling John's misery but full of assurance from the Lord, the kind of peace that comes from years of experience.

Karen and John went for their run. John was bigger and stronger, but his body was near exhaustion so he didn't push Karen too hard. He kept at her pace. They ran together a lot when they were dating. It was a great cheap date, followed by coffee and long conversations. They were so busy these days that they rarely had time to run together. Usually, they would fit in a workout whenever they could, but it wasn't usually together. After an hour run they jogged up in front of one of their old coffee shop haunts.

John asked Karen, "Do you want a cup of coffee while we're here?"

"This is kind of nice." Karen was relaxed from the exertion of the run and for a moment forgot about the previous evening's hi-jinx. "Sure, I haven't sat for a cup of coffee in the middle of the morning in ages." Immediately, Karen looked at John, worried that her comment might be insensitive of his unemployed status. "Oh John, I'm sorry. I wasn't thinking about—well, you know—how that sounded."

"I know," John replied. "I don't blame you. You have a job. You haven't lost your identity. I've just got to get another job; I can't stand not having some place I'm supposed to be." John knew he was wallowing in self-pity. He just couldn't help himself. "Usually when I run, it clears my head, but I can't get the stink of that Dumpster or garbage truck out of my head. I feel like such a loser, like I belong with the garbage."

Karen reached over and took John's strong hands in her long, finely boned ones and held them close together. She looked down at their hands as she tried to come up with the right words. It was so painful to see John suffering. She took his chin in her hand lifted it upward so she could look into John's eyes as she replied, "John, you are not garbage. You've worked hard all your life and did well in school. Then you worked harder and did well in your job. You've taken every opportunity to maximize your potential along the way. This layoff is in no way a reflection on you. You need to just accept that and not allow any other thoughts to get in your head. This layoff was mechanical, not personal. It was a numbers thing, and I wouldn't be too surprised if down the road Ford doesn't regret this decision."

She wasn't sure if she should bring this up, but decided to go ahead despite her reservations. "Do you remember when we were recruiting back in college and they were so flattering to you? Then as soon as you accepted their offer, everything became mechanical. All those calls to human resources to get things lined up on the corporate path. They were red flags to you then. I remember your wondering what you'd gotten yourself into. "Corporate policy, corporate policy" was the mantra. Whatever your question, the answer was "corporate policy." No one could think about a particular situation; they had to rely on corporate policy. It wasn't too long before you had the pad of paper out with the pros and cons columns to decide whether Ford was actually the best place for you. Remember?"

John thought back and knew Karen was right. He had questions all right; he just craved that security so much and couldn't let go if it.

"You found comfort in the corporate size of things," Karen went on. "You believed it would be safer, more money would be available. 'It's hard to sink a ship that size' was one of your comments, I think. Right? You also wanted to get a graduate degree and they had a program for that. That was a great asset then and now. It looks good to have Ford Motor Company on your résumé. They didn't promise you happily ever after. They promised you opportunity and you capitalized on it." Karen sat back and let John absorb some of the things she said.

They sat there for several minutes in silence processing these thoughts and mulling them over.

John said, "Do you need more coffee? I'm going up to get a refill."

"Sure, thanks," Karen said as she handed him her cup.

John stood and took their cups up to the counter. Karen sat at the table and fiddled with a napkin. She thought about the other offers he had back in school, mostly with banking and small manufacturing firms. John had given real consideration to these, but there was something to the prestige of Ford that made all the other jobs pale in comparison. The initial size of the offer was one thing, and they only talked to the cream of the crop. There was prestige in getting an interview with one of the big three.

Some of those small manufacturing companies had already folded under the pressure of trouble in the automotive field, so John had been partially right. He would've had some fun in the banking or finance industry but they were going through their reorganization and things looked dubious for someone right out of school. Now, with the property values in decline, everyone knew the banking industry was going to be hit hard. Pretty much everything in Michigan at this time was scary.

Growing up in the Detroit area without a father or any relatives in the car business made John look at the automotive industry with the certain awe of an outsider. This heightened the allure of a job at Ford. Karen and John had also talked about the possibilities of travel abroad, an opportunity that John hadn't had growing up with a single mom and tight finances.

There were definitely strong reasons he had decided that Ford was the place for him.

Karen took a different route in looking for a job. She wanted something small and intimate, something where she would have access to top management. John's job at Ford had allowed her to take a seemingly less secure position since she wasn't going to have to worry about supporting the family. The money was less and the benefits were limited, but she had contact with the CEO every day. Karen flourished at Cargill Electronics.

Where John was inundated with corporate policy, Cargill had virtually none. They encouraged thinking outside the box; they strove for cutting-edge proposals. It was actually the kind of environment in which John would have done well. He wanted more safety though; Cargill was in uncharted waters a lot of the time, so the propensity for failure was definitely greater.

Even though John was ahead of the curve on feminine enlightenment, he felt the burden of supporting his family. Karen always appreciated that John's family background was what fed his insatiable need for security. As frustrated as she was with John's situation, she understood why he now felt so inadequate. John walked back to the table and put the cups down in front of them.

"You were deep in thought. Any solutions?" John asked.

He watched Karen consider her answer. She smiled, "I was thinking of all the possibilities."

"Hmmm," was all that John could add.

They drank their coffee in silence for a while. John looked up and saw one of his former coworkers walk into the coffee shop. His initial reaction was to run and hide, but then it occurred to him that Larry was there in the middle of the morning, too. John stood and walked over to him.

"Larry, you too?"

"John, everyone was let go yesterday. Our old department no longer exists. Even Alan is out. Ford must be awfully desperate to cut costs to get rid of our whole department."

"Wow, Alan did say that when I was in his office, but it was all a blur. He said something about outsourcing. I thought he was making a joke since we were the ones who negotiated the outsourcing contracts. Do you know who they contracted with to do our job?"

"No, but I had several contracts in the works. I don't know what they'll do with those. It was just 'pack your stuff and get out.' I guess it's their problem. My money is not on them to be able to get it done either."

"Larry, have you met my wife, Karen?"

Karen stood and Larry reached out his hand. "It's nice to meet you, Karen, even under rotten circumstances. I need coffee, bad; last night was pretty rough. I guess I should think about getting my act together."

Karen shook his hand. "Have you made contact with anyone yet?"

He let out a huge sigh and replied, "No, I don't even have an updated résumé. Last night I hit the bar pretty hard. I've got to clear my head first."

John and Karen looked at each other and could hardly contain the laugh they were both suppressing. As bad as sitting in a bar and getting drunk all by yourself was, it still sounded a whole lot better than getting stuck in the back of a garbage truck.

Chapter SEVEN

W ELL, I'VE DONE just about everything except face reality. I guess I need to sit down, make some calls, and look at what my options are," John said to Karen as they walked back into the house. "Why don't you go ahead and go to work. I know you're in the middle of a bunch of things. We can't afford for both of us to be unemployed." John wanted some alone time to get his perspective and think things through.

Karen was thinking the same thing. She nodded her head, "Yeah, it would probably be a good idea if I put a few hours in at the office. I need to shower and dress. Do you want lunch before I go?"

"No, I'm not hungry. Besides, after talking to Larry, I'm motivated to get some things in order. I also want to talk to Dr. Brooks to see if he has any ideas." John's old advisor in grad school had been a great mentor while he was in school. "I'm sure he'll be reminded again of how glad he should be that he chose academics instead of the business world for his career."

"I'm going to make myself a sandwich. I'll make one for you, too, and put it in the refrigerator when you're ready for it."

Karen went to the bathroom and started the water. She quickly showered, dressed in a dark pantsuit with a white, open-collared shirt, and was back in the kitchen without John even realizing she'd left the room. She made the sandwiches and took hers in the car with a bottle of water to eat on the way to the office. She knew that John was in his own world and figured returning to her work might help her cope with her own feelings about the recent turn of events.

As she drove to the office she thought about their situation. "This is going to be tough for both of us. I'm already walking on eggshells. We have always been a tight couple, but something like this could tear anyone apart. I can't help wondering why John didn't call me yesterday. Why was he so afraid to let me know?"

She was glad that she had her job and a support system of good friends, but she wondered how much to tell them of what had happened over the last eighteen hours.

Karen pulled into her parking spot and walked into the building with her briefcase, her mind still processing the previous evening's events. "I never did go over the last set of contracts I took home last night; better start by reading them over again before I present them to Brad. He'll understand, but I'll bet he'll definitely take the opportunity to make a stab at Ford. He has some baggage when it comes to Ford. He's critical of them whenever possible. Oh, and I need to call human resources to find out how much it would cost to add John to my benefits plan."

Karen loved the offices of Cargill Electronics. Karen felt at home there when she had first interviewed. Even now as she entered the office, the warm, friendly, dynamic atmosphere drew her in. She looked around as she thought, "There is nothing intimidating about the setup of the office." They used soft, mellow colors like cream and moss green in the decorating, and the cubicles were set up in a circle with upper management in the middle to give employees easy access whenever anyone needed help or direction. Teamwork was the corporate mission; management firmly believed that the success of one meant success for everyone.

The property had been purchased back when land in the new suburb was cheap, so they bought a large parcel. Everything was built on one floor. The idea was to hide the hierarchy that obviously existed and communicate that management was on par with everyone. The conference rooms were off to one side to aid teams of people working together, and the break room was there as well for convenience.

At the other end of the building was the shop where engineers and electricians worked together to prepare and test projects. It was an amazing on-site laboratory. It was a long walk from one end of the building to the other, which bugged some people, but it suited the management style of the family. As an inside joke, they had a walking track, which measured a half a mile, installed around the perimeter of the building. At lunch in nice weather, you would often find employees putting in a couple of miles.

Karen sat down at her desk as some of her coworkers were returning from lunch. They were discussing a newspaper article that appeared in today's paper. Karen thought it might be the announcement of Ford's latest layoffs. She would have to let them know John was one of the unlucky to get the axe. But when they got closer, she realized they weren't talking about Ford at all. They were talking about some guy who had been rescued from the back of a garbage truck. Karen went utterly pale, her chest seized, and she couldn't breathe. This was not the part of the scenario she was prepared to discuss.

As she quickly busied herself by emptying her briefcase on her desk and acting like she was looking for something, she couldn't help but listen to their conversation. Karen couldn't believe it, but they may have lucked out. The newspaper article had not divulged the name of the victim.

Mary asked, "You look like you've seen a ghost. Are you all right? Have you been sick?" Karen and Mary met when Karen joined the staff at Cargill Electronics. Mary had started a year before and helped Karen learn the ropes of the company. Karen was exotic looking, tall and lean with long, dark hair, Mary was the opposite. She just barely edged up on five-foot-two, her sandy blond hair cut in a wedge in the back and longer in front, giving her a more mature look than her nymph-like stature and her deep, navy blue eyes exuded naturally. As all the women at Cargill, Mary dressed professionally, wearing tailored trousers and a dress shirt.

Mary gave her good friend the eye. "Do you have something you want to share with me? You hadn't mentioned that you wouldn't be in this morning. I thought we were going out to lunch and you were going to help me car shop, remember?"

She looked at her friend and decided to just let her know what had gone on. "John was laid off at Ford yesterday. I spent some extra time with him this morning to make sure he was all right. I'm sorry, Mary; I forgot about our lunch plans. Didn't Lisa tell you I wouldn't be in today though? I did call earlier." Lisa was the young receptionist at Cargill, barely into her twenties now. Hired right out of high school to answer phones and greet clients, Lisa now attended the local community college to further her education.

"Yes, of course Lisa told me, and I went ahead and made other plans. I'm so sorry for you and John. What an awful time to lose your job, with the market in such bad shape." Mary stopped, embarrassed by her lack of sensitivity. "I'm sorry; I shouldn't have said that. What was I thinking?"

"Don't worry about it. It is an awful time to be job hunting. You're right. It's really scary." Then trying to sound more hopeful, Karen continued, "I think John will do all right, though. He has great recommendations and credentials. It is just a matter of time before some smart company hires him." Karen gave her a forced smile.

"How's John doing? Does he have any plans or ideas yet?"

Karen looked at her good friend and decided to stretch the truth a little. She just couldn't talk to anyone yet about how John was really doing. His reaction yesterday was so frightening. "Oh you know, he's a little upset, but he's hopeful for something better to come along. He has his MBA and knows of some headhunters. I suppose now he'll give them a chance to show him what possibilities are out there. He wasn't too interested before since Ford paid for his degree." Well, there was some truth in what she said, though it hardly reflected the real atmosphere at home.

Karen turned back to her desk; she tried to get her files organized and figure out how she could make this day productive. Finding the contracts in the pile that needed to be reviewed gave her something to focus on, and she started working.

Seeing that the conversation was over, Mary went back to her desk, truly sorry for Karen and John yet relieved that the Grim Employment Reaper hadn't visited Cargill.

Karen tried to keep her head in her work, but she kept thinking about John and what he was doing at home. "Maybe I should have stayed home to help him get organized and put a plan together, be there for him. No, that was the last thing that John wanted. He clearly wanted to be alone. When John needs some space, he always organizes me right out of his way. That's what he meant when he suggested I go to work. He wasn't concerned about my workload; he wasn't trying to be altruistic. He wanted to be home alone."

So Karen reapplied herself to her work. She knew she should probably get as much done as possible since John might need her more in the next few weeks. No more working late.

Karen looked up when she saw Brad walking toward her. Brad was in his forties and had been a member of the Cargill team for his entire career. He had sandy-colored hair that was clearly thinning and he always wore beige suits. His clear, blue, intense eyes and warm smile showed him to be a person that could be counted on when the chips were down.

He sat on the edge of her desk and asked, "So how are you? Everything all right at home?" He had gotten the message John was laid off, but decided to refrain from any Ford Motor digs, at least for the moment.

"I'm OK. I guess you've heard that John was laid off yesterday. It's pretty strange around our house right now, but I'm sure everything will work out. Thanks for asking. Do you want to go over the City of Monroe contracts?" They were sitting in front of her.

Brad smiled and said, "Sure. Why don't we go into the conference room so we can spread them out?" They went to work going over every aspect of the contracts.

Brad looked at Karen after they had finished and smiled. "This is some of your best work. Has the Monroe city manager approved the deal?"

Karen warmed at the compliment. This was her biggest solo deal to date. John had been a big help, but as far as the company was concerned, this was her baby. "Yes," Karen replied, "he's ready to take it to his City Council. He's prepared each of the commissioners and doesn't anticipate any problems. We can start the work at city hall in the next couple of weeks. If this goes well, he has a few other projects in the wings as well. That place is an electrical nightmare; it could be really challenging.

If we play our cards right we could get all the work to move them into the twenty-first century."

Like Ford, Cargill Electronics started as the dream of its patriarch, in this case an upstart by the name of Dan Cargill, back in 1950. Dan Cargill served in the army during World War II and used the GI Bill to go to technical school to become a licensed electrician. After working for a few years for another local electrician, he started Cargill Electric. He married Nancy in 1952 and they proceeded to have four sons and one daughter. It was a tremendous source of pride for Dan when all five of his children chose to go into the business with him. Two of his sons had gone to college to become electrical engineers and his daughter had studied to become a lawyer. They were all committed to the family business, and it took all of their imaginations to grow the small electrical firm into the dynasty that Cargill Electronics had become by the time Karen was hired.

The name was changed from Cargill Electric to Cargill Electronics in the 1970s to communicate the diverse future they hoped for the company. Their adventurous spirit sometimes caused them to take on risky contracts that required a lot of imagination, and the company grew ahead of the curve. Their investment had paid off. They were now a premier electronics firm, not only in the Midwest but also internationally.

As technology grew, they grew alongside. They prepared business after business and home after home for the huge growth in electrical needs with the advent of the computer, cable, and of course, anything to do with fiber optics. There was great pride in their role as pioneers in solving ways to meet expanding electrical needs, a spirit that continued with each new project.

After graduating from college, Karen joined the company as a financial analyst. Karen did some research before the interview and blew away the competition with her knowledge of the company history and mission. When she started at Cargill, she performed project analysis to determine cost and profit information. Since each project was unique, she was learning the electronics business one nuance at a time. The Cargill family was impressed when she approached them about getting her MBA in contracts and negotiations.

Through her years at the company, Karen had become quite close to Susan Cargill Moore. Susan, a brilliant lawyer, was about ten years Karen's senior and was a true mentor to her. It may have been a little complicated considering she was also Brad's wife, but at a tight-knit company, it worked. All contracts obviously went through Susan, who was the entire corporate legal department. As Karen became more and more adept at her work, Brad and Susan recognized her progress and gave her more responsibilities.

There was some question about the possibility of future advancement, though, since all of top management was either family or in-laws. Karen wasn't going to worry about it as long as she didn't feel like she was hitting her head on the proverbial glass ceiling. After all, she was learning a lot about business and decision-making, and her list of contacts was very impressive. The job still did not pay as much as John had made at Ford, but her last raise had them pretty close.

Brad closed the folder in front of him and pushed it back toward Karen. He looked at her with concern and compassion. They'd developed a friendship over the almost ten years that Karen had worked for him. Through the years of working together, he witnessed the relationship Karen had with her husband—supportive, encouraging, generous, and honest. This was a good marriage, which indicated that not only was she a good decision-maker, but she was also a great team player. She hadn't disappointed him in his decision to hire her. Since Karen had completed her MBA, she had thrown herself into her work, utilizing her studies in very practical ways.

"As I said, this is good work. How many projects do you have in process right now?"

Karen replied, "Well, besides this one, which is pretty much done, I have four active projects and two that have been kind of simmering for a while. I've done some preliminary work on them, but I need more direction on what you're looking for." She smiled and added, "Some site visits would be nice, especially for that job in Bermuda."

"Did you build a trip to Bermuda into your cost assumptions?" he laughed in reply.

"Of course. You know I made the mistake of leaving out my own travel expense for the San Francisco bank project and you haven't exactly let me forget it yet." Karen added also laughing, "I learn from my mistakes, especially when I miss out on nice trips! You can count on site visits to nice places in all of my project budgets. By the way, I don't think a site visit is necessary for the coal-gasification plant in North Dakota, at least not in the winter."

Brad sighed in relief, "Karen, it's good to see you laugh despite the fact that Ford just sacked your husband along with twelve thousand other high-quality employees."

"There it is. I knew you'd get your Ford dig in somehow. What do you have against Ford?"

"Funny, you've never asked before. Well, I'll tell you. When I was in college, I sent my résumé to Ford, and they sent a nice little note back to me indicating that they thought I would do better elsewhere. I wasn't good enough for Ford."

Karen was obviously shocked. "I can't believe that. You've done so well with Cargill."

"Well, they wanted only the brightest and best; they didn't believe that was me. It was hard for me to accept a position with my girlfriend's father, but my options were limited, so here I am. What comes around, goes around. Look at them now, and look at us. I wouldn't wish them failure; that would hurt too many people. But I have to believe that their hiring practices were a little like inbreeding, and with everyone thinking alike and no one challenging the status quo, they caused some of the problems that put them in the newspapers today."

"It's kind of hard to argue against that," replied Karen. "I can see why you haven't been Ford's biggest fan. But John really liked his job there, and this has sucked the air right out of him. There was safety for him at Ford. He needed that security, especially the way he grew up. His dad died in the Middle East when John was a baby. His mom did an amazing job raising him by herself, especially with a limited education, but he didn't have the security of an intact family." She took a deep breath, not sure why she felt so compelled to defend John. "Risk is very scary to him. Now that he is an adult, he needs to work through this issue, especially with all these new feelings of being out of a job and an undefined future. John has never allowed himself to have an undefined *anything* before in his life." Karen sat back in the upholstered swivel chair as she continued.

"Fortunately, I have my job. Things may be tight financially, but I think it will be doable until he gets something new. We've been pretty sensible with our finances." She sighed and thought out loud, "We hoped to go to Europe this spring, you know, to take in some of the romantic spots as a tenth anniversary celebration. Fortunately, we haven't booked anything yet, so we don't have to go if we can't afford it. I'll be disappointed, though. All through the last year of our graduate studies, the idea of this trip kept me going." Karen suddenly realized that she was crying. There was a knock on the door.

Susan was softly knocking and poked her head through the door. "Do you mind if I come in? I don't want to interrupt anything private." Brad waved her in as Karen nodded her consent. Brad told Susan about John.

Susan gave Karen a hug when she heard the news. John had attended all the Cargill gatherings and Susan enjoyed his dry sense of humor and intellect. His tenacity over the years impressed her as well. Family was important to all the Cargills, and when Susan heard of John's background, she grew in respect for both John and his mother. "I know this is tough for both of you," she told Karen. "If there is anything we can do to help, please don't hesitate to ask. We love you like family, and we'll be here for you."

Karen looked at them and said, "I appreciate how good you've always been to me." She took a tissue and dabbed her eyes, trying to salvage anything that might be left of her mascara, took a deep breath, and continued. "I don't want John to rush into just any new situation. I want him to take this opportunity to pursue something that will really make him happy. I appreciate my job here, and it's a comfort knowing that I can support him at a time like this. I'm a little fearful for him. It's hard to watch him grieve and not know how to help. I want to give him the support that he's always given me—I just don't know what that is right now."

Susan rubbed her shoulder again and said, "Just be there for him. It's all you can do, and it's important. By the way, it's after five and maybe we should call it a day."

Karen gathered her papers, making sure they were in the proper order, and said she thought she should get home. "Susan, I will drop these off at your office on my way out. They're ready for your final review. I'll see you both tomorrow. Thanks for listening. Good night."

She walked back to her desk. Most of the other employees had already left for the day, so Karen didn't have to talk to anyone else on her way out. No work went home with her. Karen got in her car and drove home.

When she pulled up in front of the house, she thought John was out since his car wasn't there, but then she remembered the destruction of his car. Karen gulped down a sob and steeled herself to go in and face whatever she might find.

Chapter EIGHT

J OHN LOOKED UP as he heard Karen's car pull into the garage, amazed at how quickly the afternoon had gone. He had spent most of the day on the living room couch, dejected, frozen. The morning paper was filled with more headlines of job loss around the city of Detroit. He threw the paper on the floor, fearing his chances of reemployment were diminishing by the second. Pouting wasn't doing him any good; he mustered his strength, pulled up his résumé on the computer, and spent time tweaking it here and there. Finally, he swallowed his pride and e-mailed Dr. Brooks. John was stunned when seconds later the phone rang and the caller ID indicated it was Jim Brooks responding to his message.

"Hello?" John started.

"Hello, John? This is Jim Brooks; I just received your e-mail and would enjoy getting together with you."

"Thanks for calling back so quickly. I'd really like the chance to pick your brain. As you read in my e-mail, I was one of the unfortunate thousands to get eliminated from Ford yesterday."

"I have some ideas that might help. I assume you'd rather get together sooner rather than later? How does tomorrow work for you?"

"That would be great."

"All right, then. How about Barney's Pub, across from campus, say, at 11:45? That way we can beat the rush."

"Absolutely, I'll see you then. And thanks for agreeing to help me out."

"No problem. I'll see you tomorrow."

After the call, John sat back in his desk chair and allowed himself a small sigh of relief. That wasn't nearly as awkward as he imagined it would be.

Jim Brooks was the perfect advisor for John while he was in grad school. He was an energetic man in his late fifties, with a medium build and thinning red hair. Many times since he had met Jim, John thought about what it would have been like to have a father like him. This wasn't a slam to his own dad, since John never knew him, but he always felt that if his own father had lived, he might be just like Jim Brooks. When they met at the first student/faculty reception at the beginning of grad school, John knew he was the one he wanted as his advisor. He especially liked the way Jim looked intently at him when he spoke. He knew this was a guy who would be pulling for his success.

"Jim's such a good guy," John thought after their conversation. "It's not like he doesn't have anything else to do. As soon as I let him know what happened, boy, he was right there to help, a proverbial port in a storm."

John also called the insurance company and arranged to have his car repaired. Apparently, Karen had purchased the rental car clause on their insurance, another positive to grasp on to.

Even though he was thoroughly exhausted from the previous night's escapades, John stood in the kitchen leaning against the counter, trying to act as if nothing happened. The moment Karen walked in the door, the phone rang. John looked on caller ID and saw that it was his mother. He picked up the receiver as Karen looked at him seriously, trying to gauge John's mood. "Hi Mom. How was your day?"

Sharon tried to sound cheerful, but her voice still betrayed her concern. "Hi John. I was just wondering how you're doing."

He didn't want his mother to worry. "I'm exhausted, but OK," he replied. "Karen spent some time at the office today while I worked on my résumé and made some calls. Karen just walked in and she looks pretty rough around the edges."

"I thought I might drop off some dinner. I won't stay, but I thought you guys might like a night off cooking; I made lots."

John told Karen about his mom's offer and handed her the receiver. "Mom, thanks so much for making dinner," Karen said. "I really appreciate it. Why don't you have dinner with us?"

Sharon said, "Thanks, but no. You two need to relax tonight. I'll stop by in about half an hour. See you in a few."

Karen smiled at John. "Your mom is one in a million. She's dropping off dinner; knowing her, there'll be enough to feed half the neighborhood. She won't stay, though; we've been given orders to relax."

Karen walked over to John, put her arms around him, pulling him close, thinking how fortunate they were to have escaped last night, she held him tight and whispered into his ear, "I love you," as she enjoyed their closeness.

There was no rush to pull apart; it was a blessing to be together. They probably had become complacent, believing they would always have each other. The reality of losing John erased that complacency.

Karen quietly asked John about his afternoon. He filled her in on his progress. "There should be a car delivered here soon from the rental car agency. Good thinking to buy the rental clause on our insurance since my car will take probably a week to repair. Damages won't cost us anything either because we have the police report. How were things at the office?"

Karen thought about the girls talking about the article in the paper. "I don't know if you'll think this is funny yet or not, but as soon as I got to the office the girls were talking about an article in the paper. It seems some guy got himself stuck in the back of a garbage truck and needed the police get him out." Karen raised her eyes to see what impact this had on John. He looked concerned and edgy. Then she added, "But the victim wasn't named in the article. Do you think it might have happened to someone else, too?"

Seeing Karen's attempt at levity, John relaxed a little. "A support group, that's what I can start. We need a support group for people who can't stay out of Dumpsters and need rescuing." They both laughed.

Karen told him about her meeting with Brad. "He was very impressed with the deal we were able to negotiate with the City of Monroe. This is a pretty high-profile job. There are a lot of other cities that need the same thing, so it could generate a lot of work. You know, John, a lot of the ideas in that contract were yours. They were creative and original. When you talk to Dr. Brooks tomorrow, you should tell him about this."

Nodding as he thought back over their evenings the previous month working on the project, he replied, "It was fun, working together, feeding off what you told me, the issues you saw coming, what the City of Monroe wanted to accomplish, and brainstorming some unique ways of getting the job done without having to shut down city hall and disrupt business. That's probably a big selling point for Cargill. Your efficiencies brought the price down, which afforded them the opportunity to enhance the project. I'm glad Brad was pleased."

"Maybe you should come and work for Cargill. What do you think?"

John scrunched up his face and said, "I don't think that's a great idea. First of all, they're still a small company; I don't know that I want such a risky position. Second, there's a glass ceiling there, even if you don't see it yet. Think about it, everyone in management is some part of the family. I know it's been a great training ground for you, but at some point you're going to top out there as well. I think we need to branch out more, and I need to work for someone else."

Karen bristled at his opinion of the Cargills. She loved the Cargill family, and because of her good relationship with them, she believed that she could rise to top management of the company, in spite of the fact that she wasn't family. Exhausted and her energy reserves depleted, Karen turned defensive. "Well, they've treated me better than Ford treated you yesterday. I don't see them cutting employees just for the sake of making their own millions. That's a lot better than Ford. Didn't they just announce management bonuses last week?" Looking around the room as if she could see the answers, "Oh yes, it was some obscene amount in the millions. Their explanation was something along the lines of needing to retain talent, and then yesterday they decided to outsource the entire purchasing department, thinking they could do without that kind of talent. I don't get it."

By the time Karen finished her rant, she was red-faced and crying. John felt her frustration, yet he was caught off guard. Karen vocalized the thoughts that had plagued him all day, and still he didn't want to hear them. He handed her a tissue, sat back on the sofa, and thought about it.

She dried her eyes for the umpteenth time that day. Karen knew she'd crossed the line but didn't have an apology in her. She tried to change the topic. "Well, what do you think you're going to talk to Dr. Brooks about tomorrow? Are you going to ask him for help by making connections or are you going to just get his advice about what non-risky position you might be suited for?"

"I am not risk-adverse. I believe security is important. You know, it's because I take security seriously that you can work for a company like Cargill, one that could be out of business in a minute. That's why we should diversify the companies we work for. This economy is so bad; if we both work for the same company and it goes out of business, we're both out of a job." He knew he'd started the argument, and he needed to finish it. "I didn't mean to attack the Cargills. I know you're very close to them. They're good people, and they certainly have put their employees' jobs ahead of their own millions, as you say. In fact, even when they have overextended themselves—which they have—they didn't cut one single job. They take their employees' security seriously. Ford, as well as most major corporations from what I've noticed, could learn some valuable lessons from them. The corporate world seems to have forgotten that real people work for them, not just numbers on the page. Real people, with real bills to pay, generate the information used to make their business decisions, build their products, and supply their services. Except for the fact that we have a lot of Ford stock in our portfolio, I don't believe right now that Ford deserves to make it.

"As far as my conversation with Dr. Brooks, I don't know how that will go. I can't say that I'd be disappointed if he said that he knew of a position for me and I could start right away. But that's a little unrealistic. I'm bringing him my résumé to get his opinion before I send it to the headhunters. I'm looking at this as a first step." The doorbell rang just as he was finishing.

Sharon pulled the door open before anyone could get to it. "Mind if I come in?" she announced. They both looked up a little startled and headed to the foyer. "Mom, here let me help you," John said as he reached her first. Sharon came through the door laden with two large bags filled with all sorts of food containers.

"How many people do you think live here, Mom?" John laughed as he took the bags and led her to the kitchen.

"Oh, honey, you know when I'm busy praying, I cook like a fiend. I just can't stop myself. I couldn't decide what to make, so I made your favorite dishes: lasagna, beef stew, chili with some homemade cornbread, and a sweet potato pie. I've cooked all afternoon. I hope you don't mind."

Karen came in with more containers from the car. "John, there are still a few things in the car to bring in." She shook her head with disbelief. "Mom, thank you for all this food. You've made enough to carry us for months." Karen started to get three plates out of the cabinet and Sharon touched her shoulder.

"No, honey, I'm not staying. I just wanted to help. John, if you will help me with those last few things, I'm going to get on home before it gets dark. Do you think you can stay safe and out of the Dumpster—I mean out of harm's way—so I can get a good night's sleep?" She gave him another one of her winks to let him know that she was teasing.

He could see that she really was tired. "I think we could all use a good night's sleep," John replied. "I love you, Mom. Thanks for everything. Now go home and sleep. You've earned it."

Chapter **NINE**

JOHN LOOKED IN the mirror as he got ready for his lunch with Dr. Brooks. The navy suit, crisp white shirt, and red tie looked seriously professional. He had gotten a haircut that morning and, together with the shave, he sure didn't resemble the guy from the Dumpster only a couple of days earlier. The excitement of seeing one of his favorite mentors helped erase, momentarily, the crisis at hand.

Looking in the mirror, he leaned on the bathroom sink, resting on both palms, and sighed. "OK God, I really need your help here. I feel so vulnerable. I haven't asked for much over the years. I never know what to ask for. I don't know what You want from me, but right now I know that I can't go on without You. Show me the way. I am Yours. First, my mom gave me to You, and then as a teenager I said the prayer. But now, Lord, I don't know why You would want me, but I am Yours. I can make myself look good on the outside, but I am crumbling on the inside, Lord. Give me strength."

John stood there as if waiting for some audible answer. While he didn't hear anything, he did feel the burden lighten. And with that, he walked to the kitchen, grabbed his keys, and went on his way.

Jim Brooks was waiting for him at the restaurant when he arrived. As John walked to the table, he stood and shook hands. "Dr. Brooks, this means a lot to me that you agreed to see me today."

His mentor smiled at John as they both took their seats at the table. "John, please call me Jim; you're no longer my student. I'm happy to talk to you and see if we can move you into the right career. I have to be honest; I knew you wouldn't be at Ford forever. There are a lot of choices for a bright young man such as yourself. Let's get started and see what we come up with!"

The waitress came to the table and they each ordered Diet Coke, soup, and a sandwich. John handed his résumé to Jim, who took out a pen and a pad of paper and began to take notes as he read it thoroughly.

"This is a wonderful résumé of your accomplishments. I see you highlighted your fluency in Spanish. When did you become fluent?"

"I took Spanish through high school and college, but it wasn't until I spent time in college working with the migrant workers, tutoring their children in English, that I really became fluent. It started as a summer job after my freshman year, and then I kept it up every summer after that."

"That's incredible. I never knew you were involved in such a program."

John just shrugged. "It's something that seemed really important. I still get letters from some of the kids."

"John, that's very impressive. There's a lot more to you than meets the eye. Let's try to get some of that expressed here on your résumé. What kind of position or career are you looking for? I'm getting a mixed message. You don't have to answer me right this second. Let's get caught up on things."

They ate their lunch and talked about grad school, Karen, and Ford. There was a comfortable casualness between them.

"To get back to your question, I think you're right. My résumé is a mixed message. That's because I am mixed up. Obviously, I need a job. I need to call myself something other than unemployed. But at the same time, I want a position where I can concentrate on maximizing my skills. I don't want to grab at the first thing that comes along."

"Sure, John, I wouldn't expect anything different. But, tell me, how desperate are you for a job, financially I mean? How are your reserves?"

"I think we're in pretty good shape. We bought a house the year before we went back to grad school, probably at the height of property values, but we stayed within our means. We weren't greedy, and since interest rates were at thirty-year lows, we didn't do anything stupid like going for those interest-only or zero-down variable deals. We fixed in a great rate for thirty years. We've been making extra payments to shorten the amortization period, but we're not locked into doing that while I don't have a paycheck. Plus, I did get six months of severance pay, so we have a little time to scale back if we need to do more."

"You and Karen have been wise. Boy, six months is a good severance package, too. That gives you some time to work with. I think you should concentrate on getting the kind of position you really want. Don't worry about being unemployed right now. I know that's hard for someone like you. This economy is scary, but there are a lot of opportunities for young people who are looking to make their mark on the world. When you rework your résumé, that's what I would advise you to do. Really think about that mark and what you want to do with your life. You have such a window here to move in the direction you really want to go."

John picked up his napkin and wiped his mouth and hands, then placed it back on his lap. He looked up at the ceiling of the restaurant and took a deep breath.

"Jim, to wait for just the right position could take a lot of time. I haven't been unemployed since I was fourteen. Not even for a weekend. I've always had my next job lined up before I left the current one. I had to in order to buy most of my clothes and make it through college. I was very proud that I could be so independent and not burden my mother. It is a big part of who I am. Having a job always meant security to me; I feel too vulnerable without that security.

"Right now, I feel like I don't have an identity. When I look in the mirror, I don't recognize the person I see, and I don't even know what to look for. Most of the people around me didn't grow up as I did. They could always count on their parents for cash. They grew up with the identity of student. Then when they got a job after school, that became part of their identity. If they fell on their face, they could rely on their family to help them out. My mom did the best she could, but she didn't have much education. When my dad died, she had the rug pulled out from under her. She had to figure out a way to make it work for the two of us."

John went silent for a few minutes in order to regroup his thoughts. Jim waited patiently. He'd always respected John; now he knew why.

John looked back at Jim before continuing. "I feel desperate, but that is not what I want to communicate to a potential employer." He rubbed his face with his whole hand. "Jim, how do I regroup?"

Jim looked at the table and glanced around the room. "Why don't you start at the end and work backwards? Do you know what I mean by that?"

John tilted his head and shook it to indicate "no."

"Let me ask you this: where do you want to be in say, ten or fifteen years? Tell me something other than that you want to be employed," he added with a chuckle.

"I want what the Cargills have. I've always been critical of them, maybe because I've been jealous."

Jim looked confused as he asked, "Who are the Cargills?"

"Cargill Electronics, Karen's employer. They run a family business that is closely held and very successful. The dad started it as an electrician and together as a family they've grown it into a global organization."

Jim understood. "I see a couple of ways you could be jealous of this," he acknowledged. "Remember, though, they didn't start where they are today. It must have taken decades to grow the business. But you know, there are those opportunities available today, even here in Michigan. It takes foresight, guts, and a lot of patience. I think you have all of this. When you were at work, what turned you on the most during the day?"

John shook his head. "There really wasn't that much that turned me on in my old job. I was waiting to transfer to a different department. I wanted to do more of what Karen does. She analyzes potential jobs, negotiates for the company, and writes up contracts to get the work. It is a combination of financial analysis and sales. She's good at it, too. We actually talk about her job at home a lot. I like hearing about the contracts she's working on and what particular problems she's trying to solve. We brainstorm over dinner. It's fun." John realized that in telling Jim about this, he had started to smile. Then he looked at Jim and noticed that he was smiling as well.

"Now we're getting somewhere—I think we've found what turns you on," Jim observed. "You are a financial problem solver. You know, there are many directions you can take. I don't think you have to worry about moving out of state if you are willing to make some sacrifices. It will be pretty tight for a while, though. You could go into public policy for the state government—they could sure use some extra brains trying to solve their problems. And even if they don't know it, they have business problems. The university also needs administrative people to use skilled methods of analyses to give them proper direction—these also are unrecognized business problems. Think about all the companies out there that have difficult decisions to make and probably have no idea how to put the facts and figures together to get some answers. There is so much potential; the problem isn't knowing what to do, it is deciding who gets first crack at your skills."

John looked at Jim in shock and awe. How did he turn this absolutely abysmal situation into one with such hope and excitement?

"Now, we need to communicate this potential into your résumé. Do you think you see what I'm looking for now?"

John nodded, "It's much clearer now. Who do you think I should send my résumé to?"

Jim asked, "Have any headhunters called you?"

John thought about it, and realized he hadn't paid that much attention since he wasn't looking. "David Sinclair and David Rice have both called. I don't remember which companies they work for. What is this, every headhunter's name is David? Are they clones or something?"

Jim shook his head, "I know what you mean. They all have the same name, the same uniform—you know, the slicked-back hair, dark suit, crisp white shirt, power tie, and too much cologne. They aren't real players. You should talk to David Stewart. Yeah, I know, another David. More important probably, I think you should also talk to Ben Sadd at the Michigan Economic Development Corporation and Stephanie James at the university's department of entrepreneurial services. I'll e-mail you their phone numbers and addresses. You can use my name as a reference. I have a good working relationship with both of them."

"I didn't know the university had such a department."

"It's a relatively new department that deals with new products and services created by university employees on university time. When these items are ready for market, this is the department that negotiates the deal for splitting them off the university. It happens a lot in the medical sciences and engineering departments. It's a pretty exciting area. There's a lot of exposure to the big wigs there, and it requires you to be very innovative."

John asked, "Why does the university want to give up the financial rewards earned on their time and at their expense?"

"That's a good question. What they want to do is to get credit for the development and cash in so they can reinvest those funds into more research, which is what they are good at. Research is a monster that is never financially satisfied. They also get the academic credit for the advances so they can draw the most attractive researchers. Researchers beget grants and grants beget researchers. That's what makes university life go 'round. By spinning them off, they also shift the risk of the product to someone on the outside so that if it goes bust or someone comes up with something even more innovative, they haven't lost their investment."

"It sounds like an exciting group to work for. Do they find the investors, or do the investors find them?"

"I think it works both ways. Sometimes the investors are the research scientists who did the work and want part of the payoff. At that point they would have to leave the university."

"Is that a conflict of interest?"

"Do you mean because it seems they are being paid twice for their work?"

John nodded.

"That's why they have to leave the university. Remember, they are still taking on a lot of risk with their investment. Research and development is only one aspect of bringing a product to market and making money on it."

John sat back with a warm feeling about him. "I never realized there was so much exciting business out there," he mused. "I've spent so much of my time in the corporate setting and in an area of business where innovation was not encouraged, at least it wasn't in the purchasing and procurement department. Maybe I needed this push to get out of my comfort zone and see what I can do."

"Ford was a good place for you to start, John. You did get your MBA on their bill. But now I suggest you try your wings. You'll have to show your other qualities, some you may not even know are there. I think the most surprised person is probably going to be you."

"Jim, I feel encouraged. Thanks for meeting with me. Yesterday I felt like the whole world was against me, and now I feel like I haven't even met the world yet. I can't wait to get started attacking some of these possibilities."

Jim stood, picking up the bill, and reached to shake John's hand. John stood also, but when he reached out his hand it was to retrieve the bill. "Jim, I'd like to pay for this lunch. You've been so helpful to me. I can't thank you enough for giving me a new perspective."

"John, it has been my pleasure to meet with you, and it's my pleasure to pick up the tab. Next time when we are celebrating, you can pick up the bill at a nicer restaurant. Today's on me!" They walked out of the restaurant together.

Chapter TEN

JOHN HAD DINNER heated, the table set, and wine poured when Karen arrived home from work.

But driving home, Karen was nervous about what she would find when she got there. John hadn't called to fill her in on the meeting with Dr. Brooks. In her heart she knew Jim Brooks was a good guy, but maybe he wasn't able to help John.

When she walked into the house, the atmosphere was warm, happy, and the aroma of his mom's cooking reminded her of how hungry she was. This looked like a good sign. At least John wasn't lying on the couch totally desolate, which she could easily have predicted. No, this looked pretty good. Karen called out, "Hey, John, I'm home!"

John walked out of the kitchen, wiping his hands on a towel. "Hey, babe. How was your day?"

Karen looked him over from top to bottom. If she hadn't experienced the last two days with him, she would never have believed that this was the same guy who ended up in the back of a garbage truck. She was looking for a crack in the armor, but there didn't appear to be one. In fact, he almost looked like he got a promotion instead of the boot. "My day was fine," she answered, "but I have to ask, what drugs are you on?"

John laughed, "Karen, Karen, Karen, oh ye of little faith."

"Don't give me that. What happened today? Did Dr. Brooks give you some kind of happy pill to help you get over the frustration?"

"No, what he did give me was some perspective and a lot of great ideas that I think I am ready for."

"Wow, now he is the miracle worker. What kind of ideas?" She picked up the glass of wine and made herself comfortable on the sofa.

John walked over, picked up the other glass, and joined her. It was the most relaxed conversation they'd had in a long time. He didn't realize how much they pushed themselves. They hadn't had a vacation since before grad school. The wake-up call of the past three days helped put the focus on what was really important.

John spent all of dinner and most of the evening explaining to Karen what Jim had helped him realize about himself and what he needed to look for to achieve his dreams. John was excited to the core. He showed Karen how he'd changed his résumé to clearly explain his career objective. He told her about the university's program and the potential business opportunities. They put a fire in the fireplace and snuggled on the sofa. The absence of anxiety was refreshing. It was a few moments to appreciate each other and dream about the future rather than worry.

Karen smiled at her husband, "So, what's your next step?"

"Well, I'm going to send out my résumé to all the headhunters who contacted me when I finished school, even though Jim didn't think they would be very helpful. I just can't leave any stone unturned. Jim did send me the phone numbers and addresses for the guy at the MEDC and the woman at the university. That's where I will spend the majority of my energy."

"What's the MEDC?"

"The Michigan Economic Development Corporation. It's a semi-private corporation that is designed to funnel economic resources into new companies in Michigan. You've seen those Jeff Daniels commercials haven't you? It seems that there is some pressure on the state to try to keep educated workers in the state. I don't know much about either one of these groups, but at least now I think I know which way is forward."

"Sounds good. I need to get to bed. Why don't we continue our snuggling up there?"

"I'm exhausted," John replied. "I don't think I've slept for about four days now. Plus the anxiety at Ford was so thick, I don't think that I've rested in months. I told Jim that getting laid off might have been the best thing that could have happened to me."

"I'll go with that," Karen said, pulling him up off the couch and directing him into the bedroom. "I'll help you relax if you'd like."

Chapter **ELEVEN**

H ELLO, YES, THIS is John Sheppard."

"John, this is David Sinclair calling from Executive Search. I received your résumé and letter in the mail. I was excited to hear from you. I'd like to set up a meeting to discuss some of the opportunities we may have."

"Sure, that works fine with me," John replied, excited. After they confirmed the details of their meeting, John hung up, leaned back on the kitchen counter, and breathed a heavy sigh of relief. Well, Jim Brooks didn't think they would be very helpful, but at least an interview is better than no interview. He hadn't heard from anyone else, although it hadn't been quite a week since he sent out his résumés. "Baby steps," he thought, "baby steps."

John changed into his running clothes and hit the streets for a long-distance run. Running had always been great therapy for him. It was a time to clear his head and think positive thoughts. In high school he ran cross-country. It also was one of the suggestions from his severance package, under the heading of ways to prevent depression. Besides the many psychological benefits, there was no failure in running. You couldn't miss the ball or a basket, and usually you weren't tackled. There was no scorecard to measure against. You could worry about your times, but since there wasn't anyone to compare yourself to when you just hit the road, this was not an issue. He was religious about his run.

John shoved his cell phone in his pocket and started to walk to warm up his muscles. Then he headed off down the street toward the nature preserve, one of his favorite places to run. The day was unseasonably warm for November in Michigan. Usually it was cold, wet, and gray. Today, however, there was some sun and it was still in the fifties, perfect running weather.

Soon he was stripping off some of his outer clothes. He still felt great at the halfway mark, six miles down and six to go. He didn't see another person through the entire nature preserve. He loved running on the wood chips they used to line the trail. It was soft and smelled of cedar, oak, and maple with each step. All he could hear was the chirping of the chickadees and the squirrels and chipmunks squeaking away up in the trees, along with his own contribution of crunching footsteps. His breathing was nice, deep, and even—in through his nose and out through his mouth, just like he was trained.

Suddenly the rank smell of the Dumpster came upon him. It caught in his throat and gagged him. His pulse jumped up and clammy, sticky sweat encased his body. He stumbled at the assault. What happened? It was as if he were suddenly thrust back into the bottom of the Dumpster. He looked around and didn't see anything out of the ordinary. He stood bent over at the waist, trying to get his breath and figure out what was going on. He wiped his face with his hands, then rubbed them on his shirt. He was breathing rapidly. He felt nauseous, the vile smell of garbage still with him. What was it? He ran regularly in these woods and had never experienced this before. What happened?

John started to walk again down the trail, still confused. The smell went away about as fast as it attacked him. He started to run again, but the joy had left him. He was shaken, and he'd never experienced anything like this before. He looked heavenward and prayed out loud, "Lord, please help me. I need You. This is so weird. I don't understand what's going on."

As he walked, he quieted down and his heart rate began to return to a nice, even pace. He was able to start to jog again, but the joy he had been feeling was gone. Instead of finishing his run, he headed for home.

When John was a few blocks from home, he started walking to cool down. He looked at his watch and saw that it was just about lunchtime. He had told his mother that he would meet her for lunch today. Apparently she thought it would be a bad idea if he spent too much time alone. He walked into the house and was getting ready to shower when the phone rang again.

"Hello, this is John Sheppard." It was such a habit to answer the phone as he did at work.

"Hi John, this is David Stewart. I received your résumé and letter. I also received a note from my good friend Jim Brooks regarding you, and I'd like to get together."

"Well, that sounds great, when would you like to meet?"

"I have time available on Monday morning. Is nine thirty all right?"

"That would be great! I look forward to meeting you." This was turning out to be a productive morning, despite the emotional ups and downs. As John got into the shower, he was able to put the panic attack out of his mind for the time being. He left a few minutes later to have lunch with his mother at her house.

He walked into Sharon's house, came up behind her, and gave her a big hug.

"Wow, what did I do to deserve that hello?" Sharon said, smiling. She could tell that John was feeling pretty good.

"Can't a guy hug his mom without being suspicious?"

"Let me think," she paused for effect. "No, I don't think so. Spill it."

"I have two interviews set up with some headhunters—one who had contacted me when I finished my MBA and the other was a recommendation from Dr. Brooks. Dr. Brooks wasn't too hopeful for the Executive Search guy, but he thought the other one might have some good leads. I have the first one set up for Thursday and the other for Monday. So, we'll see what happens. How's your day going?"

Sharon smiled at her handsome son. She gave him a good look from head to toe. "Honey, I think you look pretty good. I want to hear about you. Are you running? How are you spending your time?"

John walked over to the refrigerator and pulled out a diet pop. He opened it and took a long drink from the can. "I'm all right, Mom. Yes, I'm running. I even put in about twelve miles today. It felt good." He placed the can on the counter and ran his hand through his hair while he thought about what to tell his mom.

"I have been updating my résumé and getting letters out. I feel like I really need to get a jump on things. Every day there are more people getting laid off, so the competition gets worse all the time. You know, when I was growing up, the only people you ever heard getting laid off were factory workers. They would loose a couple of weeks pay and then get called back. It was routine. It was one of the motivating factors to get a good education. But now, Mom, you read the paper and there are literally tens of thousands of white-collar workers on unemployment."

Sharon watched her son carefully, noticing the clouds of doubt in his dark, penetrating eyes. What words of encouragement were there? she wondered. She knew he was trying to put up a good front, but she could feel his fears and worries. What he didn't say was even more important.

"John, you've heard my story so many times. You know what an uphill battle I saw when word came that your father was killed. I had no education beyond high school. I had a tiny baby to take care of. I didn't have much debt. We couldn't qualify for any credit. I had such limited resources. Your father's life insurance through the military barely paid for his funeral. No health insurance was available to us. Those were my challenges.

"But you also know I had some assets. I had a baby to live for, to struggle for, to pull me out of my despair. I looked at you, all cuddly and warm in your little flannel pajamas, with those deep, navy blue eyes looking up at me, knowing only my love and care. When I saw you in your crib, those arms and legs that are so strong now would kick and reach for me as you giggled. Because of you, I had reason to persevere.

"Sometimes at night I'd sit and hold you long after you were asleep and let myself cry. You comforted me when I knew only grief and loss. You were my reason to live, but you couldn't be my power."

Sharon poured herself a glass of water and sat down at the kitchen table next to John. "As you know, I met Denise when I took the job at the cleaners. I wasn't too excited about the job, but they offered insurance and they were located in our neighborhood, so I could walk to work. Ruth, our neighbor across the street, offered to watch you for free while I worked. I could go to work knowing that you were well cared for, which reduced my stress.

"Denise would come over after work and talk to me while I made dinner and keep an eye on you, which quickly became a challenge. She was single and had grown up in the neighborhood your father and I moved into after we were married. She went to the church around the corner, which seemed like a growing and busy place. I walked past it every day on my way to the cleaners. It didn't take very long before Denise asked me to go to church with her. She said there was something there that I needed.

"I thought at first she meant a new husband—not something that I was looking for—so I turned her down. But she shared her love for Jesus and explained that there were many ministries going on at the church to help me in my new faith. John, I found that power that I needed. I can assure you that it is the only source for what you need."

"Mom," John interrupted, "you know I accepted Christ as a teenager, but right now, I don't feel that power. I feel lost and helpless. I feel abandoned by God, and I don't know what I did to deserve this." John realized that he had tears on his face. He quickly wiped them with his hand and rubbed his fingers on his pant leg. He thought about sharing with her what happened in the nature preserve that morning.

"I know, honey, and I know that your commitment was sincere. That is why I have every confidence that the Lord's hand is on your life, even as we speak. But you've always been a very independent person. You continuously fight having to rely on anyone else in your life. That's why you always needed a job, even when you were a teenager. It's like you never wanted to give anyone the opportunity to let you down again. And if you don't mind my saying, even in your marriage, you are great at being there for Karen, but how much do you let her do for you? I know this frustrates her sometimes; I've seen it with my own eyes."

"It's my job to take care of her. I want to do things for her that dad wasn't able to do for you. I want her life to be easier than yours. Don't you think Karen likes being taken care of?"

"Well, it's really not my place to say what Karen likes and doesn't," Sharon stated, "but I believe she wants to be there for you as much as you're there for her—an adult, two-way relationship. John, you and I were not two adults; I was the parent and you were the child. It was my job to take care of you. I believe that's how Jesus feels about us. He wants to take care of us. He doesn't want us to stay infants. We are supposed to grow and mature in our relationship with Him. It is acceptable and advisable for us to rely on Him for power, direction, strength, and of course, the big one, mercy. He loves us, even more than we love one another."

Sharon stopped and stood to prepare lunch. "We better eat before you starve to death."

"I'm famished," John said in agreement before continuing. "If God loves me so much, why don't I feel His power now?"

"You're grieving the loss of your job and the threat on your future. Just ask the Lord for His healing and go from there."

They ate in silence. John thought about the significance of what his mom had shared, and Sharon prayed that she had helped bring John back to Jesus.

After a long pause, John interrupted the quiet. "Mom, I need to tell you about something that happened this morning."

"What, honey?"

"This morning while I was running in the nature preserve I was feeling pretty relaxed, actually, rather happy after my meeting with Jim Brooks. All of a sudden the odor of the Dumpster came upon me and literally gagged me and sent me staggering. It scared me then, and it's still haunting me now."

"There wasn't anything around that would have brought that odor to mind?"

"No, nothing, I looked all around to see if there was anything there that smelled bad, but then just as suddenly as it happened, the smell went away."

"I can see how that would upset you. I don't know what it means; but I think it's indicative of how serious the whole Dumpster incident was to you and I think you should pay attention to that."

"Yeah, I know. Part of me wants to never be reminded of it again, and another part of me thinks I still have something to learn from the whole thing."

"Have you made any plans to talk to someone about what happened, I mean about everything, the layoff, mugging, and Dumpster stuff?"

"I really haven't. I've spent most of my time trying to get reemployed. I've tried not to wallow in self-pity since it happened. All I know is I was driving around like a lunatic."

"I know honey, but I still think you need to talk to someone to help you get your perspective, someone who maybe has some insight into your experience this morning."

"Normally I'd argue about this, but now I think I better listen. I can't exactly afford a shrink right now. Do you think one of the ministers at church might be able to help?"

"I think that is exactly where you need to start," Sharon said, smiling inside as she cleared the dishes. She asked John, "How is Karen doing?"

"Well, I think she is doing great at work. But, you hit the nail on the head earlier. I think she's frustrated trying to figure out how to help me. I probably should talk to someone about that, too. I don't mean to push her away, but I don't know how to let her in right now. I'm scared, Mom. I go through the steps every day to move forward, but mostly because if I don't, I think I'll fall into some abyss. Even when I was in college and I was looking for a job, there were set steps to take and a support system to fall back on. But now I'm on my own. Every time I hear a news story or read the paper about more layoffs, I break into a cold sweat. "

"I wish I could make it better for you," Sharon responded, "but all I can do is listen and encourage you, honey. I know that something will come along, one way or another. You're an amazing person. I have faith. I'm sure there are some lessons to learn along the way. Just take it one day at a time, keep positive, keep learning, and you'll come out on top. I love you so much."

"Thanks, Mom, I know you do; and I love you too. Thanks for lunch. I have to go. I'm going to call the church and make an appointment before Karen gets home from work, which will be soon since she hasn't been working late this week. Thanks for your help." He gave his mom a hug, grabbed his keys, and headed home.

When Karen walked in the door, she hung up her coat and put her keys in the dish on the table. Turning around, she tried to pick up on the vibe around the house. "I wonder what kind of day John had," she thought. Things were neat and orderly. It smelled like something was cooking in the kitchen. She couldn't figure out where John was. "Hey, John. I'm home."

John came down the stairs looking really good in his jeans and polo sweater. Built like a runner—tall, trim, strong—there was no question why she was attracted to him.

"Wow, you look so good and strong right now; it's hard to imagine that it was just last week I picked you up at the hospital."

John turned away from her.

"What did I say? I'm sorry; I didn't mean to upset you."

John stepped back and looked at her. "It's all right; it's just funny that you would say that because I had a weird experience today."

"What happened?"

John walked over to the window, and with his back to his wife he told Karen about his run and the reoccurrence of the stench. "It seems like every time I try to resume a normal life, something brings that night back to me. It's scary. I don't understand what it means. It just keeps replaying over and over again in my head."

Karen approached John wondering what to say, what to think, and how to make it go away. She decided to say nothing.

Evening fell, casting shadows across the living room window. "Hey, I'm starving. Something smells really good. What did you make for dinner?"

"I pulled lasagna out of the freezer, one of the things my mom brought over the other day. It should be ready soon. I made a salad to go with it. We don't have any good bread, but I don't think we need it, do you?"

"Not at all. All the food your mom brought over is going to add a few unwanted pounds if you know what I mean," and she pressed her hand on her stomach. It's great to come home to a home-cooked meal, though. Thanks for taking care of us. I'm going to change. Back in a few minutes."

Karen went upstairs to the bedroom and changed into her jeans. She washed her face and hands and freshened up her makeup. She didn't usually get dolled up for dinner, but she was trying to get a few smiles from John. She thought about the past week. He seemed to be making some progress, but what was the deal with this odor haunting him? She wondered how long that would last. A big part of her just wanted him better, right now. He sure was trying, but something seemed to be getting in the way. She checked her reflection in the mirror and turned off the light.

When Karen entered the kitchen, she saw that John had set up a pretty, romantic dinner for the two of them—candlelight, wine, fresh flowers. "I wonder what this means," she thought to herself.

"Is there something you haven't told me, John?"

"Well, I did get a couple of phone calls today. I have an interview set up for Thursday and one for next Monday. I don't know whether anything will pan out from them, but it is a start," he replied.

"Are they both with headhunters?"

"Yes. I haven't heard any thing from the university or from the MEDC yet. It hasn't been that long, though, only a couple of days since I sent out those letters. I really wasn't thinking that I would hear from them too soon. I made another call too."

"Who did you call? Some new idea for a contact?"

"I called Jeff Martin, the pastor at church."

"What inspired that?" she asked him.

"I had lunch with Mom today and told her about the incident at the preserve. She thinks it's something psychological, maybe from the trauma of last week. We can't exactly afford a real therapist, so I called the church. I'm meeting with Jeff tomorrow."

"I think that's great. You do need to talk to someone about all this; I don't like the idea of your trying to fix everything on your own. Someone with some experience might save us some very painful steps. With all that's happening around here with so many people losing their jobs, he might have some good ideas specific to our problem."

"For once, I didn't hesitate to follow some of Mom's advice," John said. "That's a sign right there that this is probably the right thing to do."

They cleaned up after dinner, watched some TV, and went to bed early, ready for whatever they might find themselves up against the next day.

Chapter **TWELVE**

A S JOHN DROVE to the church, just fifteen minutes from home, he rehearsed the events of the last week. He didn't want to come off as too pathetic, but he wanted to be real with the pastor in order to get the help he needed. When he arrived at the church, he was directed to go straight to Jeff's office. His office door was open, and Jeff greeted John as he walked in.

After John made the appointment to meet with Jeff, he'd gone to the church's Web site to find out a little about him. He learned that Jeff was married and the father of a new baby boy. He served the church as youth pastor and was the clergy in charge of the contemporary worship service. There wasn't anything said specifically about counseling services, but the site did mention that all clergy were available to meet with anyone at any time.

Jeff was in his fourth year at the church, a first assignment for him, and was in the process of becoming a fully ordained minister. He was a second-career clergy with a lot of insight. Instead of trying to be overly theological, he usually had that Midwestern directness that most of the congregation found approachable and useful. John noticed that Jeff kept himself in pretty good shape.

"Hey Jeff, how's it going? How's that little guy doing?"

Jeff walked over to John from behind his desk and shook John's hand. "He's great and so am I. Come on in and make yourself comfortable."

John sat and looked around the office. It was a simple office, technically not that much different from the ones he was used to, but there was something a little different that took the edge off. The walls were lined with bookshelves that were jammed with books. The furniture was not fancy but looked comfortable and inviting. Jeff opted to use lamps in the room instead of the overhead fluorescent lights that were there, giving the room a warmer, more welcoming feeling. It was a place you could bare your soul without the fear of judgment or condemnation.

John had decided he wouldn't tell Jeff the part about the Dumpster. He would just talk about losing his job and how he was trying to cope with that. But now that he was in this office, he felt a lot more comfortable telling Jeff everything.

They sat across from each other on the well-worn sofas and indulged in the usual small talk to get to know each other a little. When John was feeling good and comfortable, he started to fill Jeff in.

"This is a little weird since I haven't been active in this church in a long time. In the movies, counselors always want to start with family history and how bad their mother was. Is that what we should do?"

"John, I'm not a licensed counselor; I'm not going to make any diagnosis. I've had counseling classes as a part of seminary for this type of session. But after we talk I'll tell you if I think this is something that needs more professional help. I know a big part of your coming here is financial. If you need professional counseling, there are organizations right here in

Birmingham I can refer you to where their fees are on a sliding scale and no one is turned away for an inability to pay. I just want you to know that you are not locked in to being satisfied with me for financial reasons. You do have options. OK?"

"I appreciate your being up front with me. I don't know what kind of psychosis I am struggling with. I just know something is going on and I need to deal with it."

"Well, probably *psychosis* is a little strong. Why don't we talk for a while and see what you think you need after that."

"OK. I'll start with the events of last week. I was part of the headlines a couple of times, although my name was never used. First, I was part of the Ford housecleaning when they laid off twelve thousand white-collar workers. I didn't see it coming. I should have, but didn't. I didn't deal with the news very well. Instead of seeking comfort in the arms of my family, I drove around for hours in a daze, ending up in a bad neighborhood in Oak Park.

"There, my car ran out of gas, and while I was walking to get help, I was mugged by a gang. I ran away from them and hid in a Dumpster behind some stores. Bad timing for me—I ended up in the belly of a garbage truck, covered in trash. I'm pretty sure I was the guy who was mentioned in the newspaper after being rescued from the garbage truck by calling 911 on my cell phone. I was rescued, and technically I'm all right."

Jeff looked at him completely wide-eyed and exclaimed, "You have really been through it this week. I commend you for just being here and talking about it at all. I know very few people who would be as strong as you right now."

"Well, thanks, but I don't feel strong. I have to tell you, I feel fragile and lost. That pretty much sums it up. And I know my family sees this. They are so busy being careful about what they say and how they breathe. They're afraid I'll crack. There is still another thing that happened, and that's what made me come here today."

"Yesterday I was running in the nature preserve, feeling pretty good and getting my old confidence back after a good meeting with my grad school advisor when I was once again assaulted by the strong stench of the Dumpster. It was so strong and powerful that it literally knocked me to the ground. There wasn't anything there to prompt the smell. It was totally my imagination. I think I might be cracking up."

"Man, that's powerful. Is that the only time something like this has happened to you?"

"Yeah, I've never experienced anything like it before."

"Sounds to me like your mind is telling you something really important. Seems like somebody's trying to get your attention. You've obviously been experiencing a lot of panic and stress."

"Yeah, I need to get a handle on this. I'm the kind of guy who needs to feel in control."

"Let's talk about your spiritual life and see if that leads us anywhere. If it is making sense we can continue. You can always bail if you think you need to head in a different direction. Don't worry about my feelings. I just want to help."

"Well, my mom has always said that I'm a complicated person, nothing with me is just one thing or another. This has definitely been a career setback; but I think the spiritual component may be a bigger part of the problem. It sounds cliché, but I haven't been very faithful in my attendance at church lately. I don't pray much. Now here I am, and I know that I need more—but what?"

"Listen buddy, we all have ebbs and flows in our relationship with Christ. And usually these ebbs and flows do correspond to how often we attend church, but more accurately, they correspond to what we are putting into the relationship. Why don't you tell me about your relationship with Christ? We can start from there."

"My dad was killed in the Middle East when I was a baby. My mom was left to raise me alone with few financial or family resources. A woman she worked with shared her faith with my mom and brought her into the church. So by the time I was aware of what was going on around me, we were at church three or four times a week. Everything we did involved church friends or church activities. I was kind of raised by the church. I never questioned why we were always there because it was the only thing I knew. My mom and I both loved and trusted those people.

"When I was in middle school, I went through confirmation. At first it seemed routine, nothing new from all the Sunday school classes I'd been in all my life. But as the class continued, I felt that something more was being demanded of me, like I was being called to be a man, and this calling started by asking for more of a commitment from me. I talked to my mom and the youth pastor about what I was feeling. The youth pastor explained that Jesus wanted more of a relationship with me and that I needed to think about making a commitment to Him. I worked to figure out what they meant when they said that Jesus died for my sins so that I would be forgiven. I needed to understand that God loves me. So when I made my confirmation, I made a public statement that Jesus was my Savior and that I belonged to Him.

"I kept involved in the church youth program through high school, and I was involved in some of the Christian activities when I was away at college. When people ask me if I've been saved, I answer honestly, yes, but now I'm not sure what I've done with this."

"You have a wonderful testimony of God's love, John," Jeff responded. "I'll bet your youth pastor was excited that he had been able to reach one of his kids so powerfully. When did you first feel your relationship wasn't what you wanted it to be?"

"I'm sure I've fought off a good old-fashioned guilt complex for a long time since I pulled away from church. The problem is that it has been a long time since I've thought about all of this. It's kind of like an old college buddy that was in your life every day while you were in school, but when you graduated and moved on, you kind of left him behind." Nodding his head as he realized this truth for the first time, John repeated, "That's where I left God."

"Do you think that this experience is a kind of calling back to you? Maybe God is trying to get your attention?"

"Well, I do feel like someone is trying to get my attention," John mused. "It's as though I suddenly realize that my problems are bigger than me. But since I haven't called on my old college friend in so long, I don't have his phone number any more."

Jeff chuckled, "That's as good an analogy as I've ever heard. I would add that it is not only a matter of knowing the number, but being comfortable enough to use it. The distance some put between themselves and Jesus embarrasses some people. They think they've lost the right to call. The truth is that Jesus has always been there for us, waiting on us. We need to own our negligence, confess it, and get right back in relationship with Him."

Jeff stopped there for a minute, "That sounds pat doesn't it, and you sure didn't come here for a pat answer. The trouble is, it is that simple and it isn't. God doesn't just want us to call Him when we need Him. He craves relationship with us. This is a heart relationship, not just a head relationship. We have to do more than just know He exists; we need to know Him." He licked his lips and rubbed his chin with his hand thoughtfully before he continued, "Does this make any sense to you?"

"Well, yes, it makes sense to me that we need a relationship with God, to make it real. It's clear that I haven't had a real relationship with Him in a long time. I mean, I've spent a lot of time at other points in my life doing what I would call faithfully serving Him. Since then, I guess I've tried to do my own thing. I don't want to be a child. Do we have to be childlike in our faith in order to be in this relationship? That's really not my personality."

"In the Scriptures we are called to a childlike faith, but that doesn't mean that the Lord doesn't want us to grow and mature. Your mother wants you to grow and mature, but she doesn't want to lose her relationship with you. She wants you to be a thinking adult, but even more so, she wants you to be a feeling adult. She wants you to experience your life to its fullest, and she wants to be a part of that. It's exciting for her, and it's because of her investment in you that she cares so much. That is kind of how it is with God—only a million times more so. How do you keep your mom a part of your life now that she is not monitoring it on a daily basis?"

John nodded knowing what he was getting at. "I talk to her," he said.

"Talk to God, too, so He has a chance to have some input into how you're experiencing life. Maybe He can help you find a more fulfilling way to live it. You've heard people talking about God's will. Well, I'm here to say that God's ultimate will is that we experience His love for us, period. Do you mind if I tell you a little story? You know, that's the national pastime of pastors."

John nodded for Jeff to continue.

"When I was growing up I was involved in everything. I was a straight-A student, I was on the football team, I was president of my class for several years. When I went to college I continued the same, but instead of football, I chose drama and radio. I had quite a list of accolades, but at the beginning of my junior year, I experienced a bit of an identity crisis. I had a great résumé, but I realized I didn't know *me*. I didn't know who I was or what I wanted to do. I was empty. I called my mom and told her I needed to come home. I was so confused. I went home for the weekend and Mom and I had a long conversation. She concluded that it was time I know God. Apparently, she saw this coming and had been praying for me for quite some time. She directed me to Revelation 3:20, and it has been my favorite verse ever since." Jeff quoted the verse from memory: "Behold, I stand at the door and knock. If anyone hears My voice and opens the door, I will come in to him and dine with him, and he with Me."

"John, I think Jesus is knocking. It's up to you how you respond."

John stood and walked to the window to think. He knew that Jeff was right, and he knew that, just as in Jeff's testimony, his mom had been praying for him for a long time. This experience was no accident. Even if Jesus didn't make all these things happen to him to get his attention, he was definitely sure that he needed the wake-up call. God was calling him to a decision, just like He had when John was a boy. "I need to pray," he told Jeff.

John and Jeff knelt on the floor of Jeff's office and they each prayed silently for a long time. Then Jeff started to pray out loud, "Lord, I thank you for my brother John here. I thank you for his receptive heart and his desire to be in relationship with You. I praise you, Lord, for all You have done for us to pave the way. I praise you, Lord, for the time You have spent waiting on us and not giving up on us. I confess that we have not always been ready to hear You. We frequently turn away from you at the very times we need you most. Forgive us, Lord. Give us direction for Your will. Empower my brother John to be able to know Your will for his life and to know Your love. Lord, help John experience Your mercy and grace as he struggles forward in his job search and life search. We hand this over to You with thanksgiving and praise in Your Son's name."

John continued the prayer, "Oh, Lord, I do love You, and I am so sorry that I turned away from my relationship with You. I pray, Lord, that You will forgive me my self-centeredness. I want to be welcomed back into communion with You, Lord. Help me to live my life for You, to serve You, in Your will and through Your power. In Jesus' name, amen."

John and Jeff both got up off their knees and plopped down on the sofas pretty spent. "This has been quite a session, John. Where do you want to go from here?"

"I have a lot to process. I think I'd like to meet with you some more, if that's OK. I don't think a referral to a therapist is necessary. I know I've got more work to do, but I think we're on the right track. Is that all right with you?"

"I'd like to keep meeting with you. If at anytime you think you need more, though, please don't be afraid to say so. I want to be helpful, and the last thing I need is for you to worry about hurting my feelings or something if I am not doing the trick. I want what's best for you."

"I appreciate that. I guess we'll both have to check our egos at the door."

"Unfortunately—or *fortunately*—that is the way God works; no egos, just love, relationship, and healing. It does take a lot of the pressure off if you aren't worrying about results all the time."

They set up a time to meet the following week. Jeff walked John to the door and shook hands with him. "I'm very excited to work with you. See you soon."

Chapter THIRTEEN

JOHN SAT QUIETLY at his desk pondering his upcoming interview. This was the same desk at which he spent so many hours studying for his master's degree. Truth be known, John loved studying. It was well defined; the material was all before him; and he could spend hours dissecting, interpreting, and making it his own. His instructors were invested in his success, so he could go to them with any problems, no judgment, just help. Those were the days.

Now he had to figure out how to best present himself during interviews. It was scary this time. He was on his own, without backup. There was way more competition than before when he had the university behind him, a great name paving the way. Now, he was just one of thousands trying to stay in Michigan, trying to survive this predicament. How could he stand out in the crowd? What could he bring to the table different from all the others? John decided to go for a run to clear his head. He hadn't been running since the day in the nature preserve. It still haunted him.

Maybe today it would be better to run on the streets of Birmingham, he thought. It had been the town he loved for so long, the town that was always his home. He wasn't quite ready to head back to the park just yet.

John headed through the upscale neighborhood and thought about how he and Karen decided to buy the least expensive house in the best neighborhood they could afford. They had bought when housing prices were at their highest; they had been falling rapidly since. Nothing was selling. In fact, many of the houses were in foreclosure. That was a word that wasn't usually part of the lexicon of Birmingham. This was a community of resources, not gambles lost.

He tried to clear his head with gentle, even breathing. Since it was during the day, the only people he saw were a few out walking their dogs and some women running. There weren't too many men out. "They must all be at work," he mused, "where I should be."

This town, his town, was a pretty place to run. The sidewalks were runner-friendly, leading anywhere in town you wanted to go. Houses and yards were meticulously kept, and there were lots of green spaces like parks and triangles where three roads came together at angles. Most of the houses were your typical *Leave It to Beaver* colonials, large, spacious and well appointed. The downtown park attracted people of all ages throughout the year. It was a little chilly out when John was running, so there weren't many kids playing in the playground. The downtown area was a little busier.

John saw the library across the street and decided on the spur of the moment to go inside. He hadn't spent any time at the public library in years, maybe not since he was a kid. John walked in and was immediately greeted by one of the librarians.

"Do you need a bathroom?"

"Pardon me?" John asked, confused.

She was a little flustered, "I'm sorry; most of the time people come in here when they are out running and want to use the bathroom. I was just trying to be helpful."

"I'm fine," John answered with a smile. "Thanks anyway. I just wanted to browse around a bit. I haven't been here since I was a kid."

"Make yourself at home," she replied. "The adult section is over there, periodicals and reference materials are in the middle. The computers are in the reference section. If you have any questions, please feel free to ask." She walked back toward the front desk.

John looked around, trying to decide why he actually came in here. He started to wander through the stacks, looking at the titles of literature and then the nonfiction. He picked up a few books and scanned the tables of contents, waiting for something to hit him. What was he looking for?

Then he went into the periodicals section and looked over the selection of newspapers. They had current papers from all over the country. He had no idea that the library was so well connected. They had the *New York Times* and the *Washington Post*. He looked further and found the *L.A. Times* and both major Chicago papers, the *Sun-Times* and the *Tribune*. He saw on the news the other night that the most job opportunities were in Raleigh, North Carolina, and Phoenix, Arizona. He looked, and sure enough, the library had both of their major papers. Thinking it might be interesting to browse their employment sections, John grabbed the *Raleigh News and Observer* and the *Arizona Republic*. No one was in the reference area at the time, so he had the choice of any of the tables. He took the papers to one of the large library tables by the windows and spread them out.

After about an hour of perusing both of their employment sections, John compared his findings to one of the Detroit papers. The Detroit papers had a few specific want ads for managerial positions, but most of the ads were for healthcare workers, laborer positions, service workers, and headhunter agencies. John borrowed a piece of paper and a pencil from the desk and started to take notes. Instead of gathering information on specific job opportunities in these other cities, he wrote down all the different industries and business areas represented. What a contrast to Detroit, or anywhere in Michigan. He sat wondering whether Michigan could catch up to the progress these other cities had achieved. Then a thought hit him and he went over to the computers.

After figuring out how to log on to the computers, he googled new businesses in Oakland County. What a wealth of information! John spent the next two hours hardly looking up, investigating new business and existing business opportunities right in his own county. The information popping up on the screen gave John a sense of hope. Apparently there were still people in Oakland County trying to figure out a way to create opportunities and save the area from the total ruin caused by the auto companies or trade unions or whoever it was that was destroying the economy. Yes, John felt that was a bit cynical, but maybe he was entitled, at least in his own thoughts. But he couldn't deny that the paper seemed to indicate that there was hope.

John wrote down all the information on how to be included in a workforce development database used to lure new business opportunities to the area. He didn't anticipate that a job would come out of it, but any information was helpful. His brain was cooking on something.

Reading about the stats of the county also gave John hope. This just didn't sound like a ship on the brink of sinking. There was too much investment involved from too many sources. He practically laughed out loud with the idea that he could be part of the new Oakland County, one not dependent on the domestic auto industry. He couldn't help but note that the top emerging industry in the county was the advanced electronics and controls sector. Cargill Electronics was probably a big part of that statistic, as well as Karen's work there.

With his mood turned in a positive direction, he gathered his notes, stuck them in his jacket pocket, and hit the streets running.

Instead of just running blind to his surroundings, he was mentally taking note of the businesses in his hometown. He immediately noticed that they were not what he expected. First, there were a lot of banks and mortgage offices. Then he noticed a business supply store, which was unexpected, given that he generally thought of the downtown area as a "clothing store and ladies who do lunch" kind of area.

But when he looked around, he noticed that a good part of the city was utilized by offices, probably lawyers and accountants and a couple of public relations firms. He wondered what the attraction was for them, then he remembered that Oakland County was the fourth most affluent county in the country. His brain hadn't clicked like this in ages, maybe not since grad school. He ran a couple more miles before he returned home. He suddenly felt ready for those interviews. He wasn't some desperate dude begging for a job; he was a well-qualified, thinking person ready to turn on the world.

He spread his notes out on his desk with satisfaction. This was progress. He wasn't going to be beat by the system. He was starting to see himself as part of the solution rather than part of the problem. A shower first, then he would review his résumé again before Karen got home.

By the time she walked through the door, John had revamped his résumé. It hardly resembled the one he had shown Dr. Brooks just a few days earlier. Now he knew what Dr. Brooks was trying to get at when he said there was clarity missing in his previous draft. This newly revised résumé was specific about what John would bring to a company by way of vision, business acumen, and positive energy. He wouldn't just be some beaten-down accounts payable drone. He would exude success and, yes, energy with his business plans and analysis.

"Hey, honey, I'm home. How was your day?"

John walked out of the den and lavished Karen with kisses. "I've had a pretty good day. I went to the library today. It wasn't intentional. I went for a run, and by avoiding the nature preserve, I went into town—and there it was. It's pretty fun to have time to follow your nose and do things on impulse. I don't think I've ever done something just because it was there before." He winked at his lovely wife, who was smiling at him. "I could get used to this; you better hope I find a job soon or I just might adjust to this life of leisure!"

Karen flirted back, "Well, that all sounds good, but is there anything ready for dinner?"

John looked a little sheepish. "I kind of forgot about that. I was so excited to fix my résumé, the words were right there, and I needed to do it immediately. How about ordering a pizza for tonight? I'll be better tomorrow, I promise."

"Pizza sounds great for you since you've been running so much, but if I'm going to justify a pizza, I'm going to have to go on the treadmill for a while before dinner. Why don't you order it in about fifteen minutes?"

"Sounds like a plan," John replied as he looked at his watch to show that he would pay attention to the time and take care of getting dinner on the table. He kissed Karen again before she went upstairs.

Chapter **FOURTEEN**

THE NEXT DAY Karen and Mary were sitting at Greek Island, their favorite lunch spot, for much-needed one-on-one time. After looking over the menu, they ordered the usual—Diet Cokes and the restaurant's famous Greek salad.

The two became immediate friends when Karen started working for Cargill, where Mary had worked for a year. They didn't really interact that much at work since Mary worked in engineering and Karen was busy in finance, but when they met, they felt as though they had been friends for life. They had the same interests, in that they both loved to shop and read. They felt like they could talk about anything; no putting up a false façade to fit in. Nothing was out of bounds. Just a good ear from an attentive listener, someone good at helping you sort through your thoughts in order to figure things out.

Mary was still single. However, she just started dating a guy with some real possibility.

Karen started the conversation. "I feel like we haven't talked in ages. How was your weekend? Did you see Steve?"

"Haven't we talked since then? I saw Steve both Friday and Saturday nights, as a matter of fact. We went to the Pistons basketball game Friday night. That was incredible. We had seats right down on the floor. You could hear everything the players were saying to each other, even the refs. I haven't been to many professional basketball games, but it will definitely be hard to go back up to the nosebleed section after that. We went out with some people from his office afterward. It was fun seeing how Steve interacted with his coworkers; he seems to be just the same with those guys as he is with me. Then on Saturday we got carryout and brought it back to my house to watch a movie. It was a lot more intimate, and I felt really comfortable."

"Hot-and-heavy intimate?" Karen asked her with raised eyebrows and a smile on her face.

"No, we're not there for sure, but it was the first time we were really alone, just the two of us, for any extended period of time. It wasn't weird or awkward. He knows that I am not the type that jumps into bed before marriage, and to be honest, he hasn't suggested it. I'm not exactly sure what his experience is with this. He is pursuing me, though, and not the other way around."

"I'm glad that I didn't have to deal with any of that. I'm sure if John pressured me after I decided that he was the one I was going to marry, I would have given in. He was definitely the one with the stronger moral code between the two of us. I am glad that we waited, though. It made our wedding night so special. Some people think that you need to have sex in order to be sure that you are compatible. I don't buy that. I think if you are committed and love each other, everything else will follow. You may have to investigate what is comfortable for each, but you'll figure it out. That's what all those years of marriage are for!"

"Well, Steve and I have only been dating regularly for a few months, so we are definitely not ready to start talking about marriage yet. I am very attracted to him physically, though; drawn to him. Everything in me wants to be close, and that's a first for me. I want the kind of relationship that you and John have. I just haven't met the one before this. Steve may be the guy."

"That's fantastic! When are we going to go out, the four of us?"

Mary leaned in toward her best friend and asked, "I'd like it to be sooner than later, but how are things going for you?"

Karen nodded and smiled back, "Thanks for asking. We're actually doing all right for now. John is working hard to figure out what he wants to do for the rest of his life. He actually has an interview today with a headhunter and one next Monday. My intuition says that he isn't going to get his next job through a headhunter, though. We're in OK shape financially, for the time being at least. I think he needs to develop some plan on his own and sell it to someone who needs it, directly. It's just a feeling I have. He went the corporate route last time and did well, but he has grown so much since then, really in the last week since he was laid off."

"What happened this past week?"

Karen knew she'd said too much, but Mary would understand. "I can't really talk about that too much. I can tell you, though, that the process from his feelings of devastation at being unemployed for the first time since he was something like fourteen years old to reconstructing his future has been eventful."

Their lunches arrived. Karen relaxed as she enjoyed her meal. It felt good having lunch with Mary, but she felt bad that she was withholding the most troubling information. She just couldn't share the scary details with Mary without John's permission. It wasn't her story to share; she sure didn't want to embarrass him.

"If you guys don't have plans for this weekend, why don't we get together for dinner, the four of us, so you can get to know Steve?"

"I'm sure that's fine; it would be great to have that to look forward to. After John's interview today, we may need some distraction. Why don't you count on us, and I will run it past John to be sure."

Mary looked at her friend. She could tell there was something Karen wasn't telling her. Karen was a pretty transparent person and she was definitely struggling with something, something she wasn't ready to talk about yet. Mary knew that when Karen was ready, she would talk.

"I know you have more to tell me. When you're ready, I'm here to listen. No pressure."

Karen looked at Mary wide-eyed. "How can you always tell these things? I thought I was putting on such a brave front and doing a good job at that. You're right, we have experienced some really dreadful things lately, but I'm not at liberty to share."

Mary understood. "Karen, how bad could it be? I read the newspapers, you know, there are some crazy things happening out there. You have been pretty caught up in things with John, so you probably didn't hear, but there was actually a guy rescued from the back of a garbage truck last week. God only knows how he ended up in a situation like that. You see, things could be really crazy."

Karen went completely ashen, and stared at Mary.

"What's the matter? Are you all right?" Mary asked, worried. "What? What?"

Karen started to cry. She grabbed her napkin to her face and held it there.

Mary was completely startled. "What did I say that got you so upset? You look like John walked in with another woman or something."

That comment made Karen laugh. "Oh, if it were only so simple." What should she do? She needed to talk to someone so badly. John did seem to be handling things better, and she needed to talk to him or Mary. She had held it in for too long now; it felt like she was going to blow up if she didn't let her feelings out soon. "Mary, I really need to make sure it's all right with John before I share this with you, OK?"

They finished their lunch and paid the bill. "I guess we better get back to work." Her best friend was hurting, and there wasn't much she could do about it if she couldn't talk. Mary switched into her big sister role, the one in which she was most comfortable, being the eldest of four girls in her family. "Please talk to John," she said. "It's obvious you need someone to listen. That's me! Let's have breakfast on Saturday morning when we don't need to worry about makeup and getting back to work. We can still go out all of us that night, but we need some talk therapy."

Karen was also the eldest in her family, but it felt good for someone to be taking care of her at the moment. "Thanks, Mary. You're the best."

Chapter FIFTEEN

J OHN PULLED INTO the parking lot about twenty minutes ahead of his appointment with David Sinclair, the head-hunter from Executive Search. John had googled David and found that his previous employer had been Arthur Andersen, the public accounting firm that had dissolved in the Enron scandal a few years earlier. David was a CPA and worked in their audit division when he found himself without a job. Executive Search was a frequently used firm for accounting and finance positions. Before the economic downturn in Michigan, their placement success was about ninety percent, but in recent years it had fallen to something around forty percent. He could see why Jim Brooks hadn't been incredibly positive about them. Some of that forty percent was in hiring the candidates themselves on a commission basis at very low risk for the company.

John tried hard not to get his hopes up too much; he reminded himself that this was his practice interview. His notes were well organized and he knew what he was looking for now. The question was, could he sell his ideas to anyone in Michigan? Well, he wasn't going to give up without a fight, so he gathered all his confidence and walked into the office building.

The offices were on the third floor, so he took the elevator directly ahead and pushed the button. He couldn't help but think about the last time he was in an elevator, the day that would live in infamy for him—the first time in his life he was let go from employment. Better not to think about that too much today. This needed to be positive, forward thinking, not desperate. He shook his body like a wet dog, or better yet, like an athlete ready to compete. Then the elevator door opened.

After approaching the reception desk and introducing himself, John sat on the sofa in the waiting room. David Sinclair walked through the door dressed in the uniform of the day: navy suit, crisp white shirt, red tie, and highly polished wing tip shoes. He reached out his hand to John, introducing himself. John stood and took David's hand. "I'm glad to meet you, David. How are you doing?"

"I'm doing very well, thank you. Would you like some coffee?"

"That would be great, thanks. Just black."

David signaled to the receptionist to bring the coffee back to his office and led the way for the two men. David's office was austere. There were no family pictures around. In fact, there weren't any personal items in the office at all. It appeared to be an office that anyone could use for interviews. It gave nothing away of the personality of the interviewer or any clues as to how one might approach him or her. As they sat down, David began, "I've wanted to meet you for some time now. I'm sorry it's under such unfortunate circumstances. The university sends us information on all their graduate candidates. When I read yours, I immediately thought we might have some positions for you. Do you want to stay in the automotive industry?"

"I don't have any aspirations to stay in the automotive field. Both my undergraduate and graduate degrees are in general finance. I feel that my strengths are financial analysis, which can translate to any industry. It's a matter of analyzing the financial information, being perceptive, and asking questions to determine appropriate business decisions. My work at Ford dealt with analyzing purchasing agreements in order to negotiate beneficial contracts. I have a lot of experience in real estate analysis as well as pricing programs. I love to do research, to learn as much as possible about new projects."

John and David continued to talk for the next hour. During the course of the conversation John talked about what he thought he brought to a potential employer. He talked about his ideas of what the Michigan economy needed. He even was brave enough to ask about the workforce database he read about on the Oakland County Web site. He watched David's reaction to what he was saying as well to his body language. He could tell he was making a favorable impression. John wasn't sure, though, how helpful David was going to be. He seemed to listen attentively; he shuffled his papers a lot. He also wasn't writing down too many notes. John began to have difficulty registering where the interview was heading. It occurred to John there may not be anything in those papers for him.

David was impressed with John's research and preparation for the interview. This was no lightweight candidate. David had pulled some potential opportunities before the interview, but now he felt that John wouldn't be right for any of them. Some of these had been in the file since David had joined the firm. They were all relatively basic business positions for your typical B student. John was head and shoulders above any of these spots. He would have to go back to the drawing board to see what, if anything, he could scrounge up that was more challenging.

"John, I am impressed with what you have brought to me today. I have to be honest; I wasn't expecting this. Even though you have great references and grades, we don't usually see people of your caliber. Frankly, I am surprised that Ford would let someone like you go. You have a lot to offer. I need to do some more research. I am going to talk to some of my associates who deal with less automotive-oriented companies."

"I appreciate your honesty," John responded. "I liked my job at Ford, although I was hoping to move into another department before I was let go. As you can see from my résumé, I am, or at least was, fluent in Spanish. I would love to work in an international company, or at least one interested in expanding in that area. I don't need to work for a megacorporation like Ford, just one that has a vibrant passion to learn and grow. I think I would fit into that atmosphere pretty well."

"I agree. That's exactly the kind of management you need to be involved with. A lot of people around Michigan talk that talk, they sound like they want to expand the parameters of their business, but to be honest, they usually just end up cutting expenses, pretty unimaginative. I guess there's comfort in sticking with the way they've always done business, even though they aren't having much success with the old paradigm. That's how companies like Ford lose people like you. And that's a big reason why Michigan is in the shape it is. I personally find it very frustrating. There aren't a lot of creative thinkers out there."

John sat there wondering, "Where do I go from here? There were a lot of mixed messages in this interview; 'You're bright, you have a lot of great ideas, you would be an asset to a progressive corporation,' but..." John sat there looking intently at David, trying to discern what he was going to suggest as the next step.

David, on the other hand, was looking at the now-useless pile of papers on his desk, wondering how he was going to close this interview and not look like an idiot. He gathered the papers together and tapped them on the desk to make darn sure that they were even and straight when he put the paper clip on them. "Well John, I'm going to have to get back to you to set up interviews. I could set up something for you with one of these companies," he held up the paper clipped stack of papers in his hand, "but I think you would find them quite pedestrian and, frankly, a waste of your time. That is unless you're desperate financially. In that case, I am pretty sure that any one of these firms would offer you a job. They might help out a difficult situation or at least help out with benefits."

John thought about what he was saying. Karen had begged him last night not to just accept anything. She was of the opinion that he should branch out and try something that would turn him on. Somewhere he would look forward to going to work every day. He suggested that meant maybe not staying in Michigan, but even then she said they would cross that bridge when and if they came to it. To be honest with himself, he agreed with her. He didn't know where it would lead, but he didn't want to give up before giving it a try.

"We are fine. My wife has a good and stable job, and our finances are in order. My severance runs for six months, and we have savings if it takes longer than that. I know things in Michigan could get worse before they get better, but I'm not ready to just jump at anything quite yet. We have already arranged to buy my health insurance though my wife's company since it was a better plan than the COBRA offered through Ford."

"That's great. Most people who come to see me are far less prepared than you. I will get with you soon with some more appropriate interviews. How would you feel about relocating somewhere outside of Michigan?"

"My wife has a great career that motivates her. We would be hard-pressed to consider moving out of state at this point."

"I thought that's what you'd say. Well, I'll keep looking. Good luck, John. It was a pleasure meeting you." He stood and reached out his hand to John in closing the interview.

As John walked back to his car in the parking lot, he tried to figure out how the interview went. He was pretty sure that David was not going to come up with a great job opportunity for him. Now he had to remind himself that this was what he expected and not to be disappointed.

Chapter **SIXTEEN**

K AREN AND JOHN sat quietly at dinner that night. They
picked at their food distractedly, each staring off into
space. No one knew what to say first; they both had so
much on their minds. Karen looked over at John trying to figure
out how his interview had gone that day. It must not have been
too encouraging since he hadn't volunteered anything yet.

Their dinner was the last of the frozen gifts left by her
mother-in-law. She was such an excellent cook, but Karen was
pretty sure that John hadn't tasted a single bite of his dinner. If
she blindfolded him right now, he probably couldn't even tell
you what he'd eaten. Karen sat back in her chair and sighed.
John just kept moving his food around on his plate, lost to the
world around him.

"Well, when are you going to fill me in? What happened
today?"

"What? Oh, I'm sorry, honey. What did you ask me?"

"John, how was your interview today?"

"Uneventful."

"What does that mean, exactly?"

"My interview was pretty much what Jim Brooks thought it would be. The interviewer, David Sinclair, didn't have anything for me right now. He brought some possible jobs for me to interview for, but he didn't even give them to me at the end of the interview. He said I was too good for them. He called them his 'B student' job offerings. If I was desperate, he would line up interviews for them, but he really didn't think I would be interested. I declined the interviews, remembering what we talked about last night. I think I blew him away; whether that's bad or good, I'm not sure. But, the bottom line is that I came out of the interview with nothing in hand and just an 'I'll call you if I find something suitable.' I'll be honest with you, even though that's what I truly expected, I would rather have walked out of there with a job interview. I was so excited when I started the interview; I probably came on too strong."

"Oh, honey, this was your practice, remember? Dr. Brooks told you they handled too many low-end positions and that's not where you should be looking. You aren't right out of school; you are an experienced professional with an excellent education. You have the interview with that other headhunter on Monday, remember? Isn't he the one that Dr. Brooks thought would have more possibilities? If you feel you might have come off a little too strong, why don't you talk to Dr. Brooks about how you handled this last interview and get his opinion?"

"Yes, I keep telling myself this. But, without a job in hand, I can't help but feel desperate for something. I wish I would hear something from the university or the MEDC."

"Is that the Michigan Economic Development Corporation?"

"Yes, and that's where I really see myself working and flourishing. I can't think of anything more exciting than looking at start-up opportunities and seeing what can develop. I think it would be great to be part of the industry that will turn

Michigan around; especially after suffering the humiliation of being laid off."

John was definitely starting to brighten with their conversation. What started out so dark, moody and depressing was actually turning into one of the most hopeful conversations they'd had in a while. Karen felt better about asking John if he would mind her sharing what they were going through with Mary.

"I had lunch with Mary today."

"Oh, yeah, how is she? Is she still dating that guy? What is he? A lawyer?"

"His name is Steve, and yes, he's a lawyer, a patent lawyer, I think. Mary and I think it's about time the four of us go out for dinner so we can get to know him a little. What do you think? Maybe Saturday?"

"I'd be glad to go out and get away from everything. Saturday's fine."

"I was also wondering if it would be all right if I shared with Mary some of what we've been going through. I haven't said too much yet because I hadn't talked with you about it, but I really need somebody to talk to and Mary is my best friend. She can be trusted to keep confidences. What do you think?"

"I have Dr. Brooks to talk to, my mom, and you, of course. I understand that you need to have someone to open up with, and I trust Mary. So I guess it's all right with me. You can talk to her about anything you need. You've been so careful around me lately; I was beginning to wonder if you were still human." John walked over to Karen and pulled her up from her chair. "I love you. Thanks for being so supportive. I hate being in this position, but I'm glad I have you. Now let's watch our illustrious cheerleader governor tell us how she's going to save jobs in Michigan so that this economy turns around! Her speech should be on pretty soon."

Karen and John went into the living room and turned on the TV to watch the governor's "town hall meeting" on the economy. Karen hoped beyond hope that she would have some bold initiative that would bring jobs back to Michigan and get this economy turned around so that bright people like John and so many others would be able to prosper there and not have to move somewhere else. John was thinking the same thing, but in addition, he was hoping to hear specifics, maybe about the Michigan Economic Development Corporation and how they would be used to bring in more business.

The governor came on the stage. She shook hands with all the politicians attending the conference and went to the podium looking like the picture of optimism. She griped both sides of the podium and leaned into the microphone as if she were leaning toward the viewer personally. The stage was set for drama, but acting could only take her so far. Many were looking for real answers to their real problems. Platitudes will not pay the bills and send the kids to college.

John and Karen curled up on the sofa for the whole hour. They became more and more frustrated. It sure seemed the only thing that Governor Jennifer Granholm was promoting was herself. Her major solution to the problem of companies leaving Michigan and the wholesale layoff problem was investing in an educated workforce.

John finally stood up and started ranting, "Does she think the only people laid off are the factory workers? What about all the highly educated people that are out of a job? There are thousands of bankers, accountants, analysts, and even engineers out of work. Does she think that we should all roll up our degrees and become trained to be nurses and nurses' aids? I like to empty bedpans with the best of them, but my interests are not in medicine. I made that decision a long time ago. Even if she did the numbers, there are more unemployed people than nursing openings. These are all great suggestions for the under-educated public, and they're probably the ones who voted for her. But that is a drop in the bucket. Why can't she see it? Why can't she understand it? Geez, this is so frustrating."

Karen watched him, but did not interrupt. "This is exactly what John needs right now," she thought to herself, "to get it all this stuff off his chest." She sat there nodding her head in agreement. She threw in a few "uh-huhs," "you bets," and "that's what I think" to let him know that she was listening.

John was pacing now, too. He was really revved up, agitated, red, and excited. He was standing up, then sitting down, rubbing his face, then the back of his head. "Its like all the politicians have given up on us. Don't they know what potential is here? There are so many educated people ready and willing to work, a workforce in the tens of thousands to make anything anyone could imagine."

"There's still a lot of money in Michigan. Look at our sports teams! They are supported. That means money, Karen! We already have universities and colleges that are at full enrollment. Sure, more people could get a college education, but we have resources coming out the wazoo. We are in a great location with ports for shipping. And don't forget that that there are a lot of facilities available, and not all of them are out of date. A little retooling and they would work. What is standing in the way of making this state great? That is the question that we should be asking. It wasn't that long ago that Michigan was working. We were called the Rust Belt decades ago and were able to pull out of it and get new industry, computer companies, pharmaceuticals—you name it. Why are they all pulling out now?

"We even have major companies building their headquarters in Detroit. If there ever were a city that could have given up hope, that is one; but look, GM moved their headquarters there, and so did Compuware. That Karmanos guy is really smart. Do you really think that he would have invested so much in a dying place like Michigan? Well, do you?" John looked at Karen for a response.

She sat there beaming at him.

"What, why are you smiling like that?"

"You are more exciting to listen to than the governor. I don't know what she does when she goes on those trips to bring in more business, but she couldn't be a better salesperson than you. What's standing in the way of Michigan's recovery?"

"I think people are scared. People think we need to bring business in from the outside in order to make it. That may be true. But in order to bring in big business, we need to act like successful people. We need to look like the party everyone wants to attend. You know, sometimes you have to act the part before you can become the part. Act like you believe, act like you like it, act like this is the best place to live and work. After that you start to believe, start to like it and it becomes the best place to live and work. The governor thinks that she needs to give everything away to entice new business to Michigan. What she needs to do is treat everyone to a fair playing field on a permanent basis, that way both business and people will see longevity here. I can't believe giving tax abatements to new business and raising taxes for everyone else is the answer. We need a low cost structure to compete in the global marketplace. Michigan could be the place to provide this. It could and should be exciting, not desperate."

Karen walked over to John, "Man, you need to keep that passion when you talk to the MEDC people. I think you're on to something. Have you heard anything from them yet?"

"No, I haven't. But I think I should contact them again. I sent my résumé to them before I did that research at the library. I might also talk to Jim Brooks again as to whether he can call his contacts at the university for me. I haven't heard from them yet, either. I have an interview on Monday with that other headhunter, and that is all I have set up so far. I feel like a stallion trapped in a stall, rearing, trying to escape and make something of my life, but I'm so limited at the same time by these walls around me. I need to make my résumé stand out so that they pay attention, even if they don't exactly have any positions open at this time."

Chapter SEVENTEEN

MARY ARRIVED AT Little Daddy's early Saturday morning for her breakfast with Karen. She wanted to make sure they had a booth so they could eat and talk. Karen had said she had a lot on her mind that she needed to share with Mary. There was a booth in the corner that was perfect, out of the way, private, yet she could see when Karen arrived. The hostess didn't want to seat Mary until they were both there, but Mary begged her for the booth. The waitress, seeing how important it was, said she would bend the rules for her "this time." Mary ordered coffee while she waited.

Karen was a sweetheart and had been such a good ear for Mary over the years of their friendship. Mary had shared relationship issues—Karen was always there for her. When Mary's mom had breast cancer—Karen was there. It was a treat to be able to return the favor for her best friend, and she wanted Karen to be able to let it all out.

Mary liked John; she considered him to be a great guy. It was obvious how much he loved Karen, though he wasn't the easiest person to get to know. He certainly got your attention with his tall, dark, and handsome looks, but he was always serious, quiet, kind of brooding. Many Friday nights had been spent trying to get him to relax, have a little fun, let his hair down.

As Mary got to know John, she found him to be serious, an introvert. But on the other side, he was an authentic friend, someone you could count on no matter what. He read a lot and listened to NPR. He was interesting to talk to because he was knowledgeable on a lot of subjects. Mary thought about whether she ever saw him excited. She wondered if he even had any friends of his own. Who did he talk to? She perceived him as a sort of solitary person, aside from Karen, of course. Maybe he should get a job as an FBI G-Man. It matched his persona. She could only imagine how difficult it could be around their house if he truly was depressed. She thought about how hard that must be on Karen.

Just then Karen walked up to the table. "I'm sorry I'm late. How long have you been here? This table is perfect."

"I don't know, a little while I guess. I thought something out of the way was in order."

"Thanks, I need to talk. My head is messed up; I need to lay it all out and with someone who won't judge John. He is trying so hard to move on and get his life on the positive track. I'm proud of him, but watching this process is so hard."

The waitress brought coffee, took their breakfast orders, and disappeared, leaving Karen and Mary wondering where to start. Mary broke the ice. "I hope that seven o'clock is all right with you guys. I made reservations at Sweet Loraine's for dinner for the four of us. I'm excited for you to get to know Steve."

When they finished setting up the details of their double date that night, Karen began to shift in her seat and play with her silverware. She needed to get started on the real reason for the breakfast date. The noise level of the diner was increasing as the crowds grew. Karen looked at her friend and jumped right in.

"Mary, you know that John lost his job last week. Well, there is more to the story than just a simple layoff. Do you remember that article in the paper you guys were talking about, the one where the man was rescued from the back of the garbage truck?" She looked over at her friend to see if that triggered a memory. Seeing a spark of comprehension, Karen continued. "That was probably John; that is, unless someone else was rescued from the back of a garbage truck that night. When John lost his job, he was so upset that he got in his car and drove all over the place in a blind fog. He ended up running out of gas in a bad part of town, getting mugged, and hiding in a Dumpster. While he was in the Dumpster, the garbage truck came and picked up the garbage, along with John. I had no idea where he was during most of this time and was panicked at home. I spent the night calling hospitals and police stations to no avail, until finally several hours later I received a call from the hospital and his mom and I picked him up." Karen said all this in rapid succession, as it had played in her head over and over again over the past week and a half. She took a moment to drink some coffee and gave Mary a chance to catch up. She sat there waiting for her friend's response.

"Wow, I had no idea that you could make a layoff so exciting. I'm kind of blown away. Gosh, John must have been scared to death! How is he?"

"Well, to tell you the truth, I don't know. That's my frustration. He isn't letting me see how he really is. Every night when I get home, he seems to be pretty good. He goes through the motions of trying to reestablish his work life. He has some great ideas and is refining and researching them. He's trying to make contacts through his grad school advisor and some head-hunters. But that doesn't tell me how he really is. There's dinner on the table most nights when I get home. He's also keeping up with his running; some of his runs are long-distance, so I know that takes up a good part of the day."

"Karen, it sounds like he is doing all the right things, not that you'd expect anything else from a guy like John. What makes you so concerned?"

"Maybe it's just me, but it doesn't seem like he is letting me in. He seems to need to take care of this by himself and either doesn't need me or is protecting me or something. You see, he didn't call me when he lost his job; he just went driving around like an idiot endangering himself and everyone else on the road. I think he talks to his mom a little, and I know he has talked to a pastor at his mom's church. I guess I feel left out. I feel like I don't know what is going on with him. And, I really don't like that feeling."

"Hmmm, do you feel like you need to fix the problem?"

"Well, yes. I do have that urge to analyze the problem and try to fix it. But more importantly, I want to know what is really happening in him. I want to know what he is really feeling so that I can at least be a part of the solution. How can I support him through this if he won't be open with me?"

Mary thought about how to respond to her friend's frustration. Now it was her turn to fiddle with the silverware for a few seconds. "How do you like to be supported?"

Karen wasn't sure at first. That was a tough question. Sometimes she wanted to be held, and other times she wanted to be left alone. "I just want to be understood. Most of the time I want him to be there and hold me. And he has always been there for me. I can't even think of a time in my life that I couldn't count on him for support. But John hasn't needed me the same way. We talk about things, bounce ideas off one another. I like that.

"I know John struggled a lot as a kid, growing up without a dad," Karen continued. "But by the time we met, he pretty much had a routine worked out with his mom and hasn't needed much support since then. I guess he's kind of a loner. He always worked his butt off in school, at least high school through grad school, earned top honors, and had companies vying to give him a job. He's always had a job, too, since he was fourteen. You know, he graduated from college with no debt even though his mom worked two low-paying jobs as a secretary during the day and doing catering at night. Between them they paid for whatever wasn't covered by scholarships. He always has a plan for everything.

"I came from a fly-by-the-seat-of-your-pants kind of family and was in awe of how John and his mom managed. My mom would've loved being married to a guy who planned how he would achieve his dreams and wants rather than my dad, a get-what-you-want-now-and-think-about-how-to-pay-for-it-later guy. She did a lot better the second time around, and now she knows the kind of security I do. Even though we just lost John's income, honestly Mary, we are in pretty good shape financially. I know that sounds weird. This is not about financial distress. This is worse; it's personal."

Mary was trying to absorb everything Karen was saying. There was so much she hadn't learned in their nearly ten years of friendship. It wasn't like they had a superficial friendship. She felt like she could share anything with Karen. Some of this stuff just never came out before.

Mary reached across the table to touch her friend's hand. "I have a tremendous amount of admiration for John. I doubt if he's trying to shut you out of this situation, but you need to be up front with him about how you're feeling. Some guys think they are sharing when they are really staying in that protector role, and that's not what you really want. I've always looked at the two of you as a team. Actually, it's what I've been looking for in a relationship. I wouldn't worry that you're not there for him. Right now, it just needs to be on his terms. Whom did he speak with at your mother-in-law's church?"

"It was that young Pastor Martin. Do you know him?"

"I've been going to your mom's church lately, and I go to the service that Pastor Martin preaches at. I have to tell you he is an incredible person. I was hoping he was the one John was seeing. I think he could be a big help. He's a second-career pastor and has been around the block a little. I've found him to be pretty insightful."

"How long have you been going there? I thought you went to that mega community church."

"Actually, I made the switch about six months ago. I started going to the Community Church when I decided to try going back to church. I was so frustrated with the direction my personal life was going, I needed to meet new people and was invited by a guy I was seeing for a while. I liked the contemporary music and the relevant sermons and kept going even after I stopped seeing him. It's such a big church that you don't have to run into people you don't want to see. I went there for a couple of years, but never felt like joining. I joined a small group and did a Bible study. I really learned a lot. Then the service started feeling too big and too impersonal; it didn't feel like home to me, so I decided to try something different.

"Previously, I might have just used that as an excuse to stop going to church all together, but I changed there and wanted God to stay the center of my life. I looked around and noticed that the Methodist church closer to my house advertised a contemporary service on Sunday nights. It was kind of an unusual time for service, but I like it because it's a time of day that can feel lonely to a single person. I tried it, and I have to tell you, I love it. The music is the same quality of current Christian music, and the sermons are just as Christ-centered and relevant. But they have managed to make the setting much more intimate, even though they meet in a gym-like room.

"I've met a lot of wonderful people, too. In fact, that's where I met Steve. They have the same small-group format, so I've switched to one of theirs. When I switched churches, I didn't intend to switch small groups, but it's hard to stay comfortable in a small group when you are the only one who goes to another church. I picked a group of single professionals. It seems a bit strange to pick a spiritual group by demographics, but I guess the system works, because when I went to the first session I met people at the same point in life as me, with the same goals and the same concerns.

"We discuss books. You know, you get a very thorough insight into people when you discuss things like literature and issues as they're brought out in a book. It's a great way to really get to know people. Steve is in my group, so we've had very candid discussions. That's probably why we've gotten to know each other so well so quickly. It's much more interesting than the usual questions—'Who do you work for? Where are you from?'—beginning most relationships. It's been a good change for me. I feel really comfortable."

Karen smiled at Mary. "You know, you've been trying to get me to go back to church for a long time. I don't know why I've fought it so long. It might be a good time for John and me to give this a try. Does John's mom go to this later service?"

"No, I haven't seen her there. I think she goes to the traditional services in the morning. Would it be a problem to go to the same church?"

"Not really. I just think it would be good for John and me if we went to a place of our own. You know, though, we were married at that church. I'll talk to John about it."

"Gosh, look how long it's been!" Mary noticed. The breakfast crowd had thinned out considerably.

Karen looked at her watch and found that they had been there for over two hours. "We are going to have to leave an enormous tip. It was nice of her to let us talk and not to hurry us."

"Karen, I hope I've been some help. You can always talk to me, you know. I love you, and I love John, too."

"Thanks for being there. I do feel better. Just being able to express my real feelings has been such a relief. Now we can just have fun and check out Steve tonight. I'm looking forward to it."

They stood and hugged. Walking out of the restaurant and toward their respective cars, Mary smiled at Karen, "See you at your house tonight at six thirty."

"See you then!" Karen drove away feeling the weight of the world off her shoulders.

Chapter EIGHTEEN

KAREN STOOD AT the bathroom vanity finishing her makeup when she looked over at John. She tilted her head and smiled at him. "You look great, honey. Are those new jeans?"

John shook his head, "No, I haven't worn them for awhile. I guess I was starting to put on a little weight. Now that I am back to exercising regularly my clothes are fitting better. These were my favorite pair maybe last year. So what's this guy like?"

"I assume you mean Steve. I don't know a lot about him. Let's see, he's a lawyer. He goes to church with Mary; that's where they met. That may be all that I know. They should be here in about ten minutes, so I guess we'll find out a lot more tonight."

John gave Karen a hug from behind and whispered in her ear, "You look great in those jeans, too. Guess I'll wait downstairs while you finish getting ready." He gave her a flirtatious jab, turned, and left to putz around the kitchen while he waited for Mary and Steve to arrive.

John was wiping the kitchen counter with a dishcloth when he noticed the odor. At first he thought it was something around the kitchen, so he reached into the cabinet under the sink for some cleaner and sprayed the counter. The odor seemed to be getting stronger and stronger. No matter how hard he scrubbed, it wasn't getting any better. So, he got out the bleach, rolled up his sleeves, and really went at it. Five minutes later, when Karen walked into the kitchen, she was dumbfounded to find John working up a sweat as he vigorously scrubbed the entire kitchen.

"Oh my goodness, honey! What are you doing? What's wrong?"

John looked up at her, tears streaming down his cheeks. "You don't smell it, do you?"

Karen looked at him, full of compassion, totally unsure about how to help him. "Is the Dumpster smell back?"

John dropped to the floor. Leaning against the cupboards, he drew his knees to his chest and sobbed into his hands. "I don't think I can go tonight. I came down here feeling pretty good, actually relaxed, about going out tonight, even though I don't know what I have to talk about with anybody. The minute I walked into the kitchen, I was filled with anxiety. The odor—the Dumpster stink—came over me, and now it won't go away."

"Do you still smell it?"

"It's all over me! Don't you smell it?"

"John, I don't smell anything. Don't you want to go out tonight?"

"I thought I did. Oh, I don't know. I thought I did; I was worried about it. What am I going to talk about with Mary's friend? I don't have anything going on in my life that I want anyone to know about. My life stinks."

"Honey, if you want to cancel, we can. I know Mary will understand. But I believe it will go better than you think. You have a lot going for you to talk about. You haven't even been out of work for a couple of weeks yet. It's not like you can't speak English anymore. I think we should go so you can see how good your life is and how much you have to offer.

"Mary and Steve are a great opportunity for this. Mary is a very close friend and sensitive to what's going on with us. And I think this guy she wants us to meet must be someone very special too. Besides, you can avoid the topic of work as much as you want. Talk about sports or whatever. Ask a lot of questions about him so he's doing most of the talking. That way we get to know him and he thinks we're really great listeners. But it is whatever you want. I understand."

They were both sitting on the kitchen floor holding each other tightly when the doorbell rang. Their heads shot up. "Well, what should I tell them?"

John looked at his wife apprehensively.

"I'll give it a shot. But, honey, if things aren't going well, will you help me get out of there?"

"I'll keep my eye out for if you seem to need to leave, but I really don't want to push you if you aren't comfortable."

"OK, let's get the door. Or, maybe you should get the door while I run upstairs and run some cold water over my face."

Karen went into the living room to answer the front door. John watched her leave, closed his eyes, and let out a huge sigh. He had to prepare himself for what he anticipated was going to be a very difficult evening ahead. It took all the energy he could muster to get to his feet and head upstairs.

"Hey, Mary, come on in. You must be Steve. I've been looking forward to meeting you. Welcome." Karen held out her hand to shake Steve's. Then she gave Mary a big hug.

"Karen, yes, this is Steve. Where's John?" Mary looked around the room, a little concerned that she didn't see John.

Besides, Karen sounded so unnatural. A handshake for Steve? That seemed a little cold.

"Oh, he'll be right down." Karen glanced up the stairs to see if he was on his way yet. "Why don't we sit down in the living room. I'm sure John will be here in a minute." Then Karen called up the stairs, "John, Mary and Steve are here."

Karen sat and looked at her friend appreciatively. "We are only about fifteen minutes from the restaurant, so I'm sure we'll be fine with our reservation." The situation seemed so awkward. Why couldn't she think of anything to say to Steve? All she could think about was John and how he was going to make it through the night.

Karen smiled at the two of them kind of awkwardly, "I'd offer you a drink, but I think John will be right down."

Steve walked around the living room and made himself at home on the sofa. "Karen, this is a great place you have. How long have you lived here?"

Karen, relieved to have something to talk about, replied, "I guess we've been here four years. Before we went back to grad school, we were looking for a home in a great neighborhood where we could start building some equity. We spent just about every weekend for a couple of months scouring the papers and open houses looking for just the right place. We actually had a lot of fun looking and figuring out which one would be our dream house. We even went to a lot of places that were way beyond our means. You know, just to dream."

Mary smiled at the ease of conversation between her two favorite people, but was still concerned as to why John hadn't joined them yet. She imagined this could be a difficult night for him. Determined to help him as best she could, Mary silently offered a prayer for God's hand in their evening and that John would feel encouraged and supported by them. When she refocused herself on Karen and Steve's conversation, she heard John coming down the stairs.

John walked into the living room wearing a fresh shirt and looking newly clean. Karen was sure that he had taken another shower while they waited. "Hi, I'm John. Sorry to keep you waiting."

Steve stood and walked over to John and shook his hand. "It's great to meet you. Mary has told me so much about both of you. I've been looking forward to tonight."

What started as an amazingly awkward night was getting into a friendly groove. Mary hadn't told him anything about John and Karen's situation, but she was starting to get the impression that tonight was going to be a special night for all of them.

John looked at Karen, "Which car shall we take?"

Karen wondered if they should each take their own cars so that if John needed to leave they could. She was a little befuddled.

Mary ventured forward, "Steve, why don't we drive? I think we're parked behind them in the driveway anyway."

"Sure, that would be fine. OK with you?"

Karen and John exchanged glances. Then John went to the closet to grab their coats. "Sure, that's fine," he said.

Karen chimed in, "Let's go. I'm starved."

On the way to the restaurant, Steve resumed the conversation started in the living room. Maybe it was the lawyer in him, but both Karen and John were amazed at his skill in making them feel comfortable. Karen was sure that Mary had given him the heads up on their situation. Mary said she wouldn't, but maybe she changed her mind, deciding that things would go better if Steve knew what was going on.

"Say John, do you follow the Pistons?" Steve asked as an icebreaker.

"Sure, their preseason is looking good. I think they have a good chance this year of going all the way in the playoffs."

"At least we have the Pistons to root for after another disappointing Lions season."

"Some things never change, do they? I don't think we've been able to cheer for the Lions since graduating from college."

"Yeah, it's been quite a drought all right. Where did you go to school?"

"Karen and I both attended the University of Michigan for both undergrad and grad school. Where did you go, Steve?"

"I went to Albion for undergrad and Northwestern for law school."

"What kind of law do you practice?"

"I'm in intellectual property. It was a great way to marry my science background with law. It's really fun, too, since you get to see new things all the time. It's a growing field in Michigan as well. Kind of different from most of the state right now."

"Intellectual property—that's a way of saying you work with patents, isn't it?"

"Yes, I spend a lot of time at Michigan these days. A lot of patents are processed out of their research departments."

"I was doing some reading on that myself the other day. Southeastern Michigan seems to be a hotbed of research and technology."

"You know it, man. If we could get the rest of the state and the government to focus on that potential, we could eliminate most of the negative headlines."

At the restaurant, Karen pulled Mary aside. "Did you tell Steve about John's job situation? I thought you weren't going to."

Mary shook her head, "I swear, I didn't say a thing to him. And to be honest, I've never seen him so outgoing with new people. He's usually warm and kind, but much more laid back. This is a side of him I've never seen. I'm not sure what to make of it."

As the women looked on in wonder, fascinated and astounded, the guys were going on about something as if they were the ones who were old friends. Karen couldn't even think of another time she had seen John so engaged with anyone so quickly. They ordered a bottle of wine and some appetizers. Karen thought they might as well make a night of it. It was reassuring to see John enjoy being with other people, talking like the old John, full of confidence and excitement. She smiled over at Mary, who seemed to be equally encouraged with the progress of the evening.

"You must think that I was dramatizing John's reaction to the whole job situation."

Mary shook her head, "No, I think there is something very special happening here, and I think there's a bit of divine intervention going on."

Karen agreed. "Well, it's not like there haven't been a ton of prayers said on our behalf. Why would it surprise me that maybe, just maybe, someone did care about what's happening to us?" But what really amazed her was the difference from the scene back at the house to the guy laughing and enjoying the night now. This was certainly something to think about.

By the time dessert and coffee were being served, John was actually talking to Steve about losing his job. Karen squeezed her hands under the table to release the anxiety she was feeling. The evening had been such a success; she didn't want it ruined now. Karen excused herself and went to the ladies' room. Her nervousness was palatable and she didn't want to upset John.

Karen leaned back on the door to the stall and prayed, "Lord, please protect him in this sensitive subject. I know we haven't spent much time with You these last few years, but we sure do need You now. I'm sorry for the neglect, but please protect John. You know his needs; please hear our prayers. Lord, help us." Then she let out a huge sigh.

"Karen, are you all right?"

"Mary, is that you?"

"Yes, I was a bit worried about you. Once the guys started talking about work, you went pale. Then you've been in here a while, so I thought I should check on you. Are you OK?"

"I don't know. How is it going out there? I should be there for John."

"You know what? He's doing great. I think he feels like he can trust Steve, and he's been very forthright with him. Steve has been asking him questions, and John is responding with thoughtful answers. Why don't we go back so you can see for yourself?"

Mary put her hand on her friend's shoulder as they walked back to the table. When they approached, John smiled up at Karen, as if to tell her that everything was all right. Karen returned the smile and rejoined the table.

"Hey, honey guess what? You know the person at the university who deals with new ventures and inventions, the same one Dr. Brooks was trying to put me in touch with? Well, Steve does a lot of work with her, on the patent side of things. Steve was just telling me that with this push from the state government for new industry for the state of Michigan, this area has been getting a lot of attention and they need help. Steve thinks he can introduce us, perhaps put in a good word for me."

"John, I think that the best thing to do would be to get you together with Stephanie James," Steve explained. Looking at

Karen and Mary, he continued, "She's the department head who connects project teams at the university with venture capitalists on the outside. She's brilliant, and from the load of work I've been getting from her, I'm sure she would find it beneficial to have her own financial guru. She has been functioning as more of conduit at this point, but if they had their own in-house analyst, I think they would be in a better position to know what projects to sit on and which ones to promote. The problem though is that this position doesn't exist now. But I don't think it is a big sell job to convince them this is what they need."

Turning back to John, Steve said, "I think from our conversations, you would find this work very satisfying."

"I have to tell you, Steve, this sounds like it would be a dream job." The excitement in John's voice was apparent. "How hard do you think it would be to convince the university though that this is what they need?"

"Well, it seems like a no-brainer to me, but the university is a big bureaucracy. Sometimes it's harder than it should be to get things done. You know the old adage about government work. But, I know the kind of things that you could be working on, and I think it would be worth pursuing."

"Well then," John held up his coffee cup as if to toast, "let the pursuit begin!"

Mary and Karen sat there dumbfounded. What had happened here? The evening had started out so weird and with such strain. It seemed like a bust before it had even begun, but it turned completely on its ear. All they could do was raise their cups and return the toast and the encouragement.

As they were driving back to Karen and John's house, Steve went for the grand prize question. "What would you two think of joining Mary and me at church tomorrow? We go to the five o'clock evening contemporary service. There is a band with some great music, and the pastor usually has a wonderful sermon, something you can take away and use. I know there is that forty-eight hour rule before asking for a second date," and he winked at Karen, "but we could even get a bite to eat afterward, too."

John jumped right in. "I think I'd like that. What about you, Karen?"

Karen felt a little put on the spot, but she had to admit it sounded like something they should do. Hadn't she just been in the bathroom praying for assistance? "Yeah, that sounds like a plan. Should we meet there? The church is kind of central to us."

John looked at Karen, "How do you know which church it is?"

"John, they go to your mom's church. That much I have talked to Mary about before. I believe the pastor is Reverend Martin. I've heard great things about him from Mary and from your mom."

John told Mary and Steve that he'd been meeting with Reverend Martin since his job loss. "I'd love to see him preach. I'll bet he'll be surprised to see me actually at church."

When they got back to the house, the two couples said good-bye for the night. John and Karen were standing on their front porch with John's arm draped over Karen's shoulders. "What an evening," John said to Steve and Mary. "It's been a long time. I know that Karen and I really needed this. Thanks for getting together with us." It seemed ages since John felt a part of the human race and able to be himself. It had been a real evening, no hiding the stench that invaded him since loosing his job. Steve didn't seem to judge him.

John wondered, if the situation were reversed, would he be able to treat someone in his position with such understanding? Honestly, he usually thought people got what they deserved; if they were out of work, there was a reason for it. If they struggled with finances, they probably were foolish with money. That's what was so hard about being in his position. Despite always trying to do everything right, he now fell into that category. Either his paradigm was wrong, or he was that loser.

But Steve didn't treat him like a loser. He had great ideas and connections. It sounded like he was willing to make some calls for John.

Chapter NINETEEN

KAREN AND JOHN sat together in church for the first time in years. This was not what they expected. Church sure had changed since they last visited. It felt kind of weird. The room the service was held in was more like a gym than a sanctuary. The folding chairs were no more comfortable than the old pews they remembered, and instead of an altar there was a stage. The stage housed a rock band and was decorated with Pottery Barn furniture and dramatic curtains to give the effect of an urban loft. There was a single candle and cross on a table acting as an altar.

The house lights went down and the worship band emerged from backstage. Steve and Mary arrived and sat next to them.

The band, consisting of a piano, a couple of guitars, bass, and drums, started the music and were then joined by three female vocalists. The music was strong and upbeat. This was not some thrown-together church band. These players were professional musicians, well rehearsed and charismatic. There was nothing stiff or put on by the singers either. They rocked to the music and brought the congregation along with them. Within seconds, the whole room was rocking, swaying, and singing. The words were projected onto screens suspended from the ceiling, encouraging everyone to participate.

The congregation consisted of people just like Karen and John. He looked over at his wife—this former Catholic, who rarely took her coat off in church, was clapping her hands and moving to the music. She looked as if they were at some rock concert. The music wasn't the usual three-or-four-verses-and-then-sit-down, either. No, these people kept singing the song over and over until somehow they knew to move onto the next song. This went on for a good fifteen minutes. John looked at the program to see how long they would continue. He wondered if they had gotten themselves into some weird three-hour service or something.

After about three songs, the pastor, Jeff Martin, came on the stage dressed in khakis and a polo shirt. No robes, no formality; he was leading the congregation as if he were just one of them. Announcements were made and the congregation became quiet while Jeff led them in prayer. They closed with something familiar, the Lord's Prayer. Jeff then announced the offering, but instead of asking everyone to give, he addressed the visitors and invited them to sit back and enjoy the music. They were not about having guests give, he explained. John and Karen were stunned. A church asking people not to give? Now that was new.

The special music provided by the band was amazing. John thought the band was good enough that he would have paid a lot for a ticket to see them in concert. Maybe they were special guests for the evening or something. He couldn't imagine the church really had this band every Sunday night. John whispered to Steve, "Do you guys get this music every week, or is this something special for tonight?"

Steve smiled and whispered back, "The band is professional, but we get them every week. Aren't they great?"

John grinned and nodded.

After the offering was taken and the music ended, Jeff returned to the stage and took out his Bible. He didn't start reading it right away, though. Instead, he just started to talk to the audience.

"I want to tell you about a couple of guys I know, kind of a current day David and Jonathan—two guys with a lot in common. For instance, they have a strong sense of love and respect for each other, approach situations the same way, and they have the same values. They love the same sports teams and relax the same way. They're attracted to the same kind of women. The same things entertain them. They have some differences, too, but they appreciate their differences. One likes to cook, while the other loves to work with his hands.

"I want to tell you the story of these friends because they challenge and bring out the best in each other. They're trustworthy with each other, so confidences can be shared. They don't have to be an island. These friendships are rare, precious. We must value them when we are blessed to be a part of them."

John sat there entranced. Words from the story stood out to him like neon lights.

Jeff stayed with his audience in the current day. "By attempting to hide our faults and shortcomings, we tend to isolate ourselves. The dedication and commitment needed to excel in business adds to this isolation. With technology providing so many tools, we can literally go months without really talking to another person if we don't want to."

The description sounded so much like his former life that it was as if he lived it himself. John didn't move a muscle. This was his life. The only difference was that he had Karen and his mom. They were, in many respects, his only really human relationships for years. It occurred to him that he hadn't spoken to any of his former colleagues since he walked out the door from Ford. Well, he did run into Larry at the coffee shop, but even then they didn't talk. They had merely acknowledged each other. He hadn't even thought about contacting anyone. For that matter, his phone hadn't been ringing off the hook either. Wow, he wondered, what did that say about his life?

When John refocused on the message, Jeff was explaining, "We weren't made this way. From the beginning, we needed companionship. God recognized that need. Think about your needs and how you want to be remembered in this life. In order for us to be the people we were created to be, we need relationship."

John's world had been one of tables and graphs, numbers telling the story of production and pricing. Most of his communications had been through e-mails and the Internet. He wouldn't know those people if he ran into them on the street. His boss had been impressed with his work, but he had never really taken the time to find out about John, what his aspirations were. They used his work—and discarded him. It was pretty easy for them to do, since they'd stayed away from getting to know him as a person.

Jeff was right. It was an empty existence. He'd been craving more, but he thought that came with accomplishment. He hadn't thought about relationship, that is, beyond Karen and his mom. Now without either relationship or accomplishment, he sure felt wasted. This feeling of isolation was powerful and was pervading his life. John understood that he needed to do something about it.

Jeff closed his message with the Bible story of David and Jonathan and their friendship. John sat there absorbing every-thing. When it was done, Karen leaned over and took his hand. "Well, did it live up to the hype?"

John rubbed his eyes as if to clear the fog. "You know, I think it did. I believe that Jeff preached that message just for me."

After the final song, a rousing chorus of "What a Friend I Have in Jesus" but definitely not sung like the version they did in church camp when John was a youth, John, Karen, Mary, and Steve stood looking at one another as if thinking, where do we go from here? Jeff walked up and put a good-natured arm on John's shoulder. "Hey buddy, I didn't know you were going to be here tonight. Welcome!"

"Hey, Jeff, that was a great message tonight. Steve said you were a good preacher, and I have to say, it's been a long time since something has hit me like that. I want to introduce you to my wife, Karen."

Karen and Jeff shook hands. "I agree—that was kind of incredible. You talked about a lot of things I've been feeling. Thanks." Karen felt a little awkward. She didn't know if it was the informality or the exuberant outgoing nature of this big preacher, but his warm smile and reassuring hug had her charmed in seconds.

Jeff turned to greet Mary and Steve. They obviously had a rapport. "It's good to see you guys. How do you know John and Karen?"

Mary gave Jeff a hug and told him that Karen was one of her very best friends, that they had met at work and hit it off immediately. She winked at Jeff, "We are your example of how important friends are, because I would be lost without Karen. She has been my confidant, advisor, and support since the day we met."

Karen smiled. "It goes both ways." Then she added, "We went out last night and finally met Steve in person. They asked if we wanted to join them for church tonight and we kind of put everything together then. This service is amazing. The music is so alive, and the congregation is an active part of the whole thing. It is so different from anything I've experienced before—

you know, the 'just show up, put in your time, and get to the coffee and doughnuts' scenario."

Jeff laughed out loud. He rubbed his stomach as he said, "Hey, don't knock those doughnuts, they worked to bring in the sinners for a long time!"

They all laughed this time. Steve piped up, "If we are going to get to dinner, we should probably get going. Jeff, I'll see you at small group on Wednesday night." He put his arm on Mary's waist as he asked, "Is that all right with you?"

Mary touched his hand, a show of intimacy that did not go unnoticed by either John or Karen. "Sure, I'm starved. How do burgers sound? How about Kelly's Bar and Grill?"

John, Karen, and Steve all nodded in agreement and said their good-byes to Jeff.

John leaned into Jeff and said, "I'll see you tomorrow for our appointment."

"I'm looking forward to it—my office OK?"

"Great. I'll be there at one o'clock."

The foursome headed to the parking lot and got into their respective cars. Karen couldn't wait to hear what John had to say. She could tell that he was just about to bust. Karen and John sat in the mustang with John in the driver's seat. He made no move to start the car, though.

"Do you know what I just realized tonight?"

"No, but I can't wait to hear."

"I have never really had a best male friend. I've had friendships—you know acquaintances, but nothing really deep or substantive. To be honest, it's not something that I spend a lot of time thinking about. Then last night, meeting Steve, I think I've met someone that I could be real friends with—the kind that Jeff was talking about in his sermon. This is what I need. I've felt so isolated since losing my job. I lost my way, my purpose.

"I've been driven to succeed since elementary school. I've always deeply respected my mom and everything she sacrificed for me. It's made me passionate to make her proud of me. All I've known is that I'm all she has. She didn't demand this of me, but I just sort of understood it to be my responsibility. This didn't give me much time to play or hang out. You know that. Karen, you were there.

"In fact, I probably wouldn't have you if you hadn't made me see how much I needed you. I can't even imagine what kind of an empty machine I would be if it hadn't been for you. I thought I could just work and work and work until I was a great success. I didn't know what I wanted to be a success at, as long as I was a success. That way all the sacrifice would be worth it. And then it was gone—done—kaput. My life was blank, but you were there. I have wonderful people in my life; you, my mom, Dr. Brooks, and now Jeff and Steve.

"I know you have Mary—you can go to her and talk. You talk to her in a way that you can't with me. You help each other figure stuff out, figure me out, figure work out. It's a wonderful thing for you. Until now I didn't think I needed that; I've never had it, so I didn't think that life rule applied to me. But I was wrong." After finishing that huge revelation, John was spent. He didn't know where all that came from. His hands were gripping the steering wheel like someone might steal it. He let go, shook his hands to return circulation, and relaxed for the first time in longer than he could even remember.

Karen turned to face John. "Well, my prayers have been answered," she responded. "As I listened to Jeff speak tonight, I thought about how isolated I felt in our relationship because I couldn't be the person that you seemed to need. I felt helpless, useless. It's been so frustrating, and I didn't feel like I could bring it up with you. I knew you needed something, but I sure didn't know what to do for you. I think a friendship with Steve will be great. I sensed an instantaneous connection between you. I'll bet it just happens."

When they arrived at the restaurant, Mary looked at Karen, "You two OK?"

"Yeah, I'm sorry we took so long—bet you thought we got lost! That was a very strong sermon Jeff preached."

All four walked into the dark and cozy tavern and sat at a booth along the wall. The waitress came to the table, handed out menus, and took their drink orders. They all sat waiting for someone to start the conversation. Karen looked at John and Mary. She smoothed her hair and adjusted the napkin on her lap. "John's mom, Sharon, mentioned that the Sunday evening service might be something we'd be interested in, but she really undersold it. I don't remember feeling like I'd been touched like that before. I loved the music, and the message hit me between the eyes."

Before she could go on, they all started talking. Apparently, Steve and Mary had felt the same way when they were first exposed to this contemporary style of worship. Talking about relevant topics, reaching people where they are, coming to the people instead of holding out for people to come to you—this is a concept that's hard to ignore, especially when people are hurting out there, lost, confused, and desperate. They were engrossed in conversation through dinner. By the time the waitress offered coffee, all four felt like they'd been friends forever.

John mentioned he had an interview the next morning with another headhunter. This was the guy his advisor had recommended, so it might have more potential than the first guy he had interviewed with. John felt like they should head home so he could prepare a little more. "After this weekend, I feel like

I'm in a better frame of mind for this interview than the last one," he said optimistically.

Steve looked John squarely in the eyes and said, "I'm going to call Stephanie James tomorrow morning and get the lowdown on what's happening and what they're looking for. I'll see if I can get something scheduled soon."

Each couple went their separate way, content that something really good had begun.

Chapter TWENTY

THE NEXT MORNING, John and Karen were getting ready for the day. They were never big talkers in the morning and each was particularly introspective on this morning. John had his interview with the headhunter and then a session with Jeff in the afternoon.

He was really looking forward to meeting with Jeff. After last night's service, John wanted to get some more input from Jeff about getting his faith on the right track. John couldn't help thinking that this was really the second time in his life when he was in a desperate situation that the church was part of his salvation.

Yes, *salvation* was the right word here, because when he was a baby, his mom was completely lost and the church was there for her. He knew in his heart that it was really more than the church that kept them afloat. It was the Lord with His hand on them, directing and protecting them and, in the truest sense of the word, saving them. Years later, here he was again, desperate, dark, and fresh out of the Dumpster; and it was the Lord again, using the situation to guide him back to the fold—saving him, even if He was saving John from himself.

Karen had a lot on her mind as well. She sat on the edge of the bed looking at her husband. "Boy, if looks could get you the job, you'd have it made," she encouraged. "You certainly look the part of a successful, upwardly mobile entrepreneur. I'd take financial advice from you any day. Come to think of it, I already do. Remember John, you have only changed paths here for a couple of weeks. Please don't think that you have to just jump at anything to get a job."

John hugged his wife and pulled her toward him. This certainly felt different than previous days. "Honey, Steve and I talked about some great ideas this weekend. I feel like I have a new confidence. I actually feel like there is a plan here. I don't know if this interview is a part of the actual plan or just a preparation for it, but I'm not worried. I'm open to see what's going to happen. I hope I feel this optimistic at the end of the day. But, honey, this is the first day in two weeks that I actually looked forward to whatever might come. That change of attitude can only help me, whether in this interview or something else. It's helping me."

They went downstairs, grabbed a quick breakfast of cereal and coffee, and headed out for the day.

Mary was already at work when Karen arrived. Karen went right over to Mary's desk and gave her a big hug. "What's that for?" Mary asked while she smiled.

"Well, girlfriend, he is a special guy!"

Mary's smile turned into a huge grin, "So you approve?"

"If he is having half the affect on you that he had on John, you are one lucky girl."

"John liked him?"

"Come on, what's there for him to not like? The guy was personable and got the evening going after those first awkward moments—and then proceeded to instill in John a confidence that's been demolished over the last couple of weeks and that was threatening to keep on destroying him. And to top it all off, he connected on a faith level with John. I know that John had already started something with Jeff Martin, but after that message, combined with the weekend as a whole, John feels like he is being cared for—that he's not alone in all this. I'm so relieved, like my own frustration level is being healed. It's not just going away, like sweeping bad feelings under the rug, which is my usual *modus operandi*, but it's really healed. I just want to thank you. I'm so grateful for a friend like you."

Mary had to wipe a tear from her eye. It was kind of hard to remember that this was their office, a place of business. "Steve's been exactly the same way with me. He just knows how to be a great friend. He's comfortable in his own skin, straightforward, and really cares about people. Our relationship isn't like anything I've ever experienced before. We've taken the time to really get to know each other, and I think it's paid off. We share a strong level of trust. I feel comfortable asking or telling him anything. Wow, you know what, I have to get off this subject or I won't get anything done today! Why don't we talk at lunch. Are you available?"

"Actually I'm not. I have to be down river late this morning for a meeting with a new client. I probably won't be back today. You know how that traffic is; I'm going to be heading back at just the wrong time. How about tomorrow?"

"Tomorrow's fine. Then I can hear about John's interview. I know Steve will be asking about it."

John arrived at his interview a good half hour ahead of schedule. When he left home, he knew it was too early, but he wanted to be calm and unrushed. Even if this didn't turn into an actual job, he wanted to make a good impression for Dr. Brooks's sake since he had made the connection. John opened the windows and turned off the car. It was a little cold out for the windows open, but he needed some fresh air and some quiet time.

John closed his eyes and prayed, "Lord, this is hard for me, but I trust You. I am in Your hands. Whatever comes of this interview, Lord, I know that You have a plan for me. You have saved me from some difficult situations lately. I trust that there is something better for me. Give me a peace that passes my understanding and help me to feel Your strength. In Jesus' name I pray, amen."

He hadn't done that for ages. It felt a little stilted at first, but soon he was on a roll and really put it all out there. When it was time for John to go in for the interview, he was ready.

David's office was on the second floor. He took the stairs up and walked down the long, empty, utilitarian hallway. The fluorescent lights in the hall, along with the pale blue paint and the commercial blue print carpet, made it look almost antiseptic. There were uniform nameplates on each office; none stood out from the rest. Without any trouble, John found Suite 205 and went in. There wasn't anyone at the reception desk, just a bell and a note to ring for service. John tapped the bell and three guys came out of three separate rooms.

All three looked as if they had been through the *GQ* Guide to Dress for Success—the same dark navy suit, crisp white shirt, red print tie, polished wing tips, and enough product in their hair to assure a perfect look for an entire day. Clones, that's what they were. It was kind of scary looking at all three of them standing there with those foolish "I don't know who you are but I'm glad to see you" looks on their faces. But that wasn't the worst. John stepped forward, introduced himself, and all three moved toward him and introduced themselves as "David." The chuckling that followed was something they had been through a thousand times, but it unnerved John.

David Stewart showed John into an interview room. John had the feeling of déjà vu. This interview was exactly the same as his earlier interview with the headhunter, with the same questionnaire-type questions and the same fill-in-the-blank mentality. The only thing that was different was that John knew he was not a fill-in-the-blank candidate. No, he had a bigger vision than that now. He could hardly wait for the interview to be over. These people weren't looking for his type, and he wasn't willing to be their type—at least not yet. Between the research he had done at the library and his conversation with Steve the past weekend, John had gained a glimpse of a bigger plan. These bozos had no clue as to what John had in mind. Maybe, John thought, it was time for him to ask some questions.

After David asked his list of questions, he sat back and looked at John. "You know, this is a really tight job market right now. We have some positions available here in Michigan, but they are at a significantly reduced level than the position you held at Ford. If you are interested in searching outside of Michigan, we have connections to several positions that we can arrange interviews for."

John was not surprised to hear this. He knew the song and dance. "David, I am not really interested in moving outside of Michigan right now. My wife has an excellent job here in the Detroit area and is extremely happy. What do you know about the Michigan Economic Development Corporation?"

David didn't expect this. "Well, to tell you the truth, beyond those Jeff Daniels commercials talking about all the opportunities here in Michigan to develop small businesses, I don't know too much. They haven't contacted us to fill any positions for them."

"No, I don't think that's how they work. Do you think there is real opportunity there, or do you think it's just some feeble attempt to generate some positive buzz for Michigan?"

"I haven't really thought about it a whole lot. Our business has been more geared to helping people move out of Michigan. There just hasn't been much demand here for our services, so we've shifted. There are so many people out of work, I can't think of the last time I placed a really quality prospect in a position here in Michigan. It's very sad."

"Yeah, that's got to be frustrating. I guess you're happy getting people employed. It's not the end of the world to have to move somewhere, for job security."

"That's what most of the people walking in here are looking for. They want security. Most of them have been through years of the threat of losing their job hanging over their heads, and they are tired. They have kids; some are supporting parents. It's really tough out there. Every day there is another announcement that another company has chosen to move out of Michigan. People have come to the resolution that they have to move if they want security. Security just doesn't live here anymore!"

"Well, I appreciate that," John said. He was really thinking about that word *security*. That had been one of the most important words to him his whole life. This situation had shaken his sense of who and where he found that security.

"John, I'd love to tell you that I have some interviews for you around here, but that's not the case. Jim Brooks spoke so highly of you that I wanted to meet you and see if there was something I could arrange with our contacts around the country. There are many areas of the country that are not experiencing the difficulties that we have around here. We could even set some things up for your wife."

John wanted to tell him right there that he felt there was a bigger plan waiting for him, but he just smiled. "David, can I take a rain check on that? I have some ideas that I'd like to pursue around here first. I guess, despite my own experience and what I read in the papers every day, I'm still an optimist."

"Absolutely. Let me know if you need me for anything. I don't want to pop anyone's bubble, but it's an uphill battle. I wish you the best."

When John was back in his car, he thought about the interview. No one was very hopeful about Michigan's prospects, but John couldn't believe that the whole state was going to fold up and blow away. There were some really smart people trying to get some things going, and he needed to hook up with them and be a part of the solution rather than running away.

He looked at his watch and wondered if he had time to stop at his mom's for lunch before heading over to the church to meet with Jeff. It was weird, but the time with Jeff was what he was really looking forward to that day. It would be worth rushing to spend some time with his mom as well, so he headed directly to her house. He picked up his phone to give her a little notice.

"Mom? Hey, I'm between appointments. Do you have anything for your poor, starving boy?"

"John, long-time-no-see! I assumed that no news was good news. I can whip up some sandwiches. How far away are you?"

"I'll be there in fifteen minutes. I love you, Mom!"

Chapter TWENTY-ONE

TIME WITH HIS mom was a refuge for John. She was the person who knew him inside and out, faults and all, the one person he trusted to love him unconditionally. Karen hadn't given him reason not to trust her, but his mom was time-tested. She would want to know what was happening in his often-worried head, but she always let him come to her on his own. She was confident that John would eventually tell her what she needed to know as well. Sharon was a very wise woman. This was the best therapy there was.

Typical of John, he ambled toward his mother's house absorbed in his own thoughts. Looking for sanctuary instead of someone to listen, he would fill her in on his own terms, the way it had always been.

John smiled at his mom and gave her a big hug. "What's for lunch?"

"I made some roast beef sandwiches. I have some chips and pickles to go with them if you're interested. What would you like to drink?"

"Do you have Diet Coke? I could use the caffeine."

"Sure, make yourself at home. How much time do you have?"

"About an hour. I had an interview this morning with another headhunter, and this afternoon I'm meeting with Jeff Martin again." He didn't even need to look at her to know that she was smiling.

John had finished his lunch and filled Sharon in on everything that had happened so far. The conversation started off slowly while John figured out where he was mentally and what he wanted to share. Sharon usually asked few questions, enough to let him know that she was really listening. By listening she learned what John felt was important and this helped her understand him better. He really didn't know where she got her patience from. It was not a gift he could reciprocate.

One of the reasons John had so few really close friends was because he and his mom had always been so close. He never needed other people to spill his guts to. This sometimes made Karen feel like an outsider, but Sharon was easy to talk to for her as well, so she kind of understood. It was one of the things they had to work through during the early the years of their marriage.

Despite their closeness, Sharon had not been able to persuade John back to the church after college. She never understood why he was so reluctant to get involved in church as an adult, but she didn't lecture him about it. He knew where she stood on the matter, and she believed he would come around in his own good time. His mother quietly prayed for years that John and Karen would get hungry for the Lord. God was always faithful in their time of great need, and here they were, back on God's doorstep.

After John had unloaded everything he had been ruminating on for the last two weeks, he sat back and took in a deep breath. "Well, what do you think?"

Sharon smiled at her handsome son. She couldn't help thinking about what his father would think about the kind of man John had become. He was especially handsome in his dark suit, fresh shirt, and tie. He was the ultimate corporate model. His eyes were intense, and he spoke with such passion. Who wouldn't take him seriously?

"John, I see that you have not wasted your time these past couple of weeks. Not only have you done a lot of research, but you've also processed these ideas into a constructive plan. This sounds exciting. Who have you talked to and what has been their response?"

"I've really only given Dr. Brooks a glimpse of what I've been thinking about," John explained. "He actually planted a lot of these ideas in my head, and then I've been trying to figure out what to do with them. The other night Karen's friend Mary and her new boyfriend went out to dinner with us. I haven't met very many of Mary's other boyfriends, but this guy's amazing. He's a patent attorney, and when I started to tell him what I've been thinking, he seemed to get it. In fact, I think he's going to try to help me contact some people around the state to see what we can get going. I didn't waste my time with the headhunters I had appointments with today telling them about the kind of things I've been thinking about. They spent the whole interview filling out their forms, and I didn't get the idea that they were the 'think outside the box' kind of guys."

"What's next in your game plan?"

"I'm headed over to the church for another session with Jeff. You know we went to church the other night?"

"Well, I didn't want to pry, but yes, I knew you went. What did you think of the service?"

"Hmmm, where to start?" He knew what his mom wanted to hear, but the pleasure of drawing this out was too delicious. "Well, it's pretty different going to church in a gym. I think they try to make it worshipful." He loved to tease his mother and make her squirm a little. "I don't know if they try, you know, a little too hard." This was hard to pull off; he was literally cracking up inside.

"Mom," he laughed out loud, "I can't do this. I thought the service was incredible. I can't wait to go back. Jeff's sermon made me sit up and take notice. The music was dynamic and right on. With the lowered lights and the casual stage set, you totally forget that you're even in a gym. I don't think it's like anything I've ever experienced before. You know, I don't think that it is better than a more traditional service, but maybe by changing the location, décor, and the music, they make it stand out so that the message has a chance to resonate as something new. I don't mean to downplay the quality of Jeff's message, because it hit me right between the eyes, but the setting helped me to hear it. It was a little like coloring outside the lines."

"So, I have to ask, do you think you'll go back? And what was Karen's response?"

"I can answer both. Yes, we will be back because it seems right for both of us. I watched Karen swaying to the music, and we talked about the sermon on the way to the restaurant afterward. I even like the time of day of the service. Sunday night seems like the weirdest time to go to church, but it works. It changes the paradigm of the whole church thing. I wondered what families with kids would think about it, but there are a lot of families there. In fact, it seemed like two-thirds of the people stayed for the dinner afterward. We didn't stay because we had made other plans; I don't think Mary and Steve wanted to come on too strong. Maybe next week we'll stay; we'll see. Hey, you know what? I have to go. It's almost time to meet with Jeff. I love you, Mom. Thanks for the lunch!"

"Keep in touch, honey. I can't wait to see how your ideas pan out."

Chapter TWENTY-TWO

EFF AND JOHN sat in Jeff's office talking earnestly about the changes John felt he needed in his life. The key to his future was getting his spiritual life back on track. He had thought about it several times over the last few years, but it always got shuffled to the bottom of the deck, one of those items that never seemed to get done, like cleaning out the attic. Who cleans out the attic anyway? The only time you really give it some serious thought is when you need something you haven't seen in a long, long time. Well, John knew this was the time to take stock.

"Jeff, I was thinking that my life since college has been kind of like the story of the man who built his house on the sand. It works pretty well while there are no storms, but watch out for the big one, because without the right foundation you'll get blown away."

"Good insight. Those old parables make a lot of sense, even today. What foundation do you think would be better?"

"So, you're not going to give me the answers? Well, I guess I'd say I need a foundation that goes down deep. You know, down through the sand, into the rock, and then deeper into the rock. I don't want to be blown away again."

"What do you mean 'through the sand'? Why don't you just move your 'house' to a stronger location?"

"Yeah, I know what you're saying. I'm not saying anything too different. I've got some wonderful people in my life. Karen, my new friends, and of course, the one person I've always had, my mother. These are not people or things I want to move away from. But they can't be my anchor anymore, either."

"I get it. That's insightful. So you feel for that anchor you need to dig deeper to reach something stronger than any of those people for the storms?"

"Yep, that's it, and I know that my anchor must be Jesus. I really want to change. For instance, I have no desire to go back to my life at Ford. It would be like putting on that old pair of shoes that have been sitting in your trunk for a few months. When you replaced them, they were the comfortable shoes and the new ones felt odd. But after wearing the new ones for a while the old ones seemed to have grown lumps and bumps in places you didn't remember. I don't have anything against Ford. For a period of time, they lived up to their end of the bargain. But they're a corporation. They needed to act and function like a corporation. Today, corporations are not like your family, a place of refuge. No, you have a job, and you do it for the remuneration that is contracted. Anything other than that is a bonus."

"I have no bad feelings toward Ford or anyone working there. It was time for me to spread my wings. I never would be here if I hadn't lost my job. The Dumpster incident directed my attention to the changes that needed to be made. My job and career had become my god. That support structure landed me in the Dumpster. It really couldn't have ended up in a more appropriate place."

Now his attention was to who his God was going to be. Yes, he knew the answer to this question, but the real difficulty lay in how to do it. This is where Jeff came in. "OK, Jeff, you've heard the whole ugly truth about me, my life, and my foils." John ran his hands through his hair, as was his custom in tight difficult situations. "How do I get where I want to go from here? I don't want the path I was on. I want to be able to be a better person. I want to be able to, you know, let go and let God. It's been so long I don't even know if I'll recognize Him if I see Him!"

"Slow down brother—let's not throw the baby out with the bathwater," Jeff reassured him. "Remember, the person you are is the one God made. He loves you, gifted you according to His will. You don't have to become something you're not for God to love you, forgive you, and call you His own. He wants your love, and He wants a relationship with you. You need a support structure you can count on. What you didn't realize is that you had one all along. You'd just forgotten and weren't using it. Bottom line: when you think all this is getting to be too much, just remember we are really only called to do two things."

John nodded as he remembered them, "Love God with all your heart mind and soul and love your neighbor as yourself. Yes, I remember."

"You also know that loving isn't a single act. It encompasses your whole life, your whole being. That's where the rest of the Bible comes in. Those biblical truths are there to show us love, to help us love, and to bring us love. But it all comes down to love. When you were a kid, how much time did you spend in Scripture?"

John thought about this. "Not much really. When I first became a Christian, I threw myself into Bible study, but I didn't stick with it. We had Scripture memorization, but I can't really pull out too many of those verses. I participated in activities, did mission trips, and prayed with other kids and adults. We spent a lot of time bonding. We heard a lot of talk. But I don't have a lot of memories of actually studying Scripture. My mom was doing Bible studies all the time when she sat at the kitchen table and poured over the meaning of various verses. The closest I came to that would be fill-in the blank booklets. I don't think I took them that seriously."

"A lot of kids don't take that style of Bible study seriously," Jeff explained. "I don't think it challenges kids very much. I do think that your Scripture memorization did stick because you just pulled up one of the most important verses in the Bible. There's a lot more depth there than you think. My point is, we are not reinventing the wheel. You have a great background to build the kind of relationship with Christ that you are searching for as an adult. Last time we met, you made the analogy that your relationship with Christ was like a friend in college that you simply moved away from. You know, many people reconnect with old friends. There's a catching up period in which you'll talk about what's been happening in your life, maybe similar to, say, confession.

"Then there is a commitment to reestablish your friendship. This is not unusual. It happens when both parties want to reconnect. It's not easy to reconnect with someone who is rejecting you, is it? Since God hasn't been and isn't likely to become the one who's doing the rejecting and you desire the relationship, you should be in great shape. I talked last night about friends and the importance of friendships. We need people in our lives to hold us accountable, to support us, and, yes, to challenge us. No one is there for us more than Christ. That's the beauty of this relationship. It is the single most reliable, credible, safe, encouraging, and reassuring relationship we can have. In fact, I believe there is no better."

"So what's the next step?" John wondered aloud.

"Well, the best way to get reconnected is to reconnect. What's standing in your way?"

John knew what Jeff said was true. He also knew that he was ready. This was so awesome. A few weeks ago he felt utterly alone. Now he was being recharged with a new and yet old relationship with someone utterly dependable. He felt moved to tears. He wanted to pray, needed to pray—and not in desperation; no, in joy. He felt like a new creature.

Jeff sat quietly, giving John time to mull over all the ground they had covered. "Some people think this is an everyday occurrence," Jeff mused, "but these breakthroughs are far and few between." Jeff knew that people just didn't walk into his office every day claiming a need and listening to Jeff just rattling off the answer like some wise rabbi.

That day's session did not mean there wouldn't be hills and valleys for John in the future. They merely reestablished his support system, so when the trials came, he would be better prepared, he would be supported. He would understand the value to his life.

Chapter TWENTY-THREE

J OHN AWOKE FROM the best night of sleep he had in the last month and put on his cold-weather running clothes. He stood looking in the mirror and wondered about the face looking back at him. There were the same intense eyes, dark hair, furrowed brow, and firmly set mouth he was used to seeing, but the face itself looked more weathered, more tired, more wrinkled. He felt like he had aged years in just a few weeks. That's what stress will do for you; it sure takes its toll. There was nothing on the docket for the whole day, so he decided to take advantage and get in a long run.

He walked into the kitchen and found Karen having a bowl of cereal and reading the paper. She looked up and smiled at him. "Hey, handsome. Looks like you're going for a run. Any route in mind?"

"It's going to be a long one, maybe twelve or fifteen miles. I'm thinking about trying the nature preserve again." He knew he was going to get a reaction from his wife for this choice.

Karen didn't fail him. She was stunned and concerned. "Do you think that's wise? It hasn't been long since the last time you had one of those episodes. I have to get to work, and I'm going to be really worried about you. I'm not sure that I can get anything done worrying about whether or not you're OK."

John knew she was right. It had been only a couple of weeks since the last time he was overwhelmed by the Dumpster stench, but he really felt like he was in a different place. "Honey, I appreciate your concern, but I need to get this thing behind me so I can move forward. If another episode occurs, I'm going to pray. I'm going to get down on my knees and pray. This run is part of my recovery and the building of the new me."

She rubbed her forehead with the tips of her fingers and looked off into space. There was so much more going on than a simple job change. John gave her a hug, "Don't worry about me. I'm in good hands." He walked out of the house and took off down the street.

Karen pushed her bowl and cup toward the center of the table, put her elbows on the table, and rested her head in her hands. She cried softly for a couple of minutes. They weren't exactly tears of sadness or worry. They were an emotional release from all the changes. As she wiped tears from her cheeks, she prayed. But this time she didn't start by praying for John. No, this time she prayed for herself. Karen turned her eyes heavenward and opened her heart.

Since she and John started dating, she was never the spiritual member of their twosome. Sure, in high school, she participated in the activities when John invited her, but the church was never hers. She always felt like a visitor. When they were in college, they had joined some of the campus interfaith groups, but again, although she knew the lingo, she never really gave her heart. After graduation, once they were married and careers were started, life just took on an excitement of its own. They didn't think about church events unless specifically invited by Sharon, and those services mostly fell on holidays. Karen knew that John understood her reluctance to join his church and to walk away from her own family traditions, which upon reflection, weren't much.

At the Sunday night service Karen had an experience of her own to think about. Despite John's current drama, the stirring of her spirit didn't have anything to do with him. The music spoke to her. The message was meaningful to her. For the first time in her life, she felt like she belonged in church. Karen could tell that John felt the same way. He was transparent in his desire to be back involved in the church. This was the first time she wanted to continue going back to that service; she wanted it more than anything. She knew this was more than what she had ever felt before. This was a beginning for her. When she opened her eyes at the end of the service and saw that John was experiencing something similar, complete joy filled her. They were where they belonged.

Sitting at the table, Karen began her first prayer not begging in a crisis but speaking with heartfelt surrender to a new best friend. "Lord, thank You, thank You, thank You for the healing that is taking place. Thank You for being there for us despite our reluctance to seek You, for waiting on us. Thank You, God, for forgiving me. My heart is so full of Your love, not just love as one of Your children, but love for me from Jesus. I'm sorry, Lord, for rejecting You for all those years."

Karen felt something else new: confession and then love, a renewed spirit. How many times in her growing up had she confessed some sin to her parents, and instead of feeling forgiveness, she felt rejection, convicted, and unworthy of forgiveness? This was a big part of why she had been so reluctant to face Jesus. She was afraid that she would not be forgiven. Now she had no choice. She needed to face her own reality. She needed Jesus in her life. She needed something bigger than herself and something way more reliable.

After praying, Karen felt an intense hunger. She was hungry to learn more. Despite all the activities she had participated in over the years, she knew very little about what the Bible actually said.

Karen closed her eyes and whispered out loud, "Thank You, Lord, for this hunger."

The whole situation had brought John and Karen to their knees, humbled them so they could see their need. The need was always there, but in their apparent success, they believed they could do all things in their own power, with their own well thought out plans, following their own well thought out rules. Now, they knew this was false. They needed someone bigger than them. Karen didn't know if God caused John to loose his job or just used the situation to bring them to Him, but at that moment, in her brokenness, it didn't matter. She was home.

Karen closed this first amazing prayer time by asking, "Lord, please give me Your direction. I want to grow in my relationship with You. How do I do this?" She had never been here before and didn't know what was next. Whatever it was going to be, she was ready. She just wanted the Lord to make His will known to her.

John ran through the neighborhood for a good twenty minutes before he was ready to venture over by the nature preserve. It would be putting it mildly to say he was nervous. He was terrified. He was putting God to the test. The real question was, who was being tested here? Was it John and his faith or the Lord's love? It didn't matter; one was going to meet the other, and it was frightening but necessary for him. John felt an encouragement to run into the preserve. He took a deep breath and entered.

John loved to run in the cold, crisp weather. It was invigorating and cleansing. The leaves that had fallen on the path crunched with each graceful, purposeful step forward. The leaves were mostly off the trees by then and the sky was gray, and the words to a familiar song kept going through his head. He kept up his normal pace. He didn't see any other people running this particular morning, and the solitude suited him just fine. He could hear his own breathing and the wind in the branches. He was particularly aware that he was approaching the spot on the trail where he had encountered the stench. Not conscious that he had stopped running, John started to walk, waiting for something to happen. Then without thinking, he was down on his knees. He felt reborn, new and different than the guy who fell asleep in the Dumpster, different from the guy rescued by the police from the back of a garbage truck. He wept as he prayed, "Thank You, God, for my redemption. I am not worthy. Thank You, Lord, that You love me more than I love myself, before I deserved Your love. This must have been how Paul felt on the Road to Damascus."

He also knew that like Paul, his story wouldn't end there. Jesus had a plan for his life, and John knew that it was going to be more amazing than anything he would have imagined because his imagination was limited by his human vision. John whispered to Jesus, "I love You and want to serve You. Please use me according to Your will. I am done with my small-time plans. Whatever You have in mind, I am Yours."

John got to his feet, brushed off the sticks and bark from his clothes, and looked around at his surroundings. It didn't look the same any more. At first he walked in awe of how the Lord had reached out to him, and then he began to run again. He ran with a new fervor, with a new power. He knew this represented the new power in his life, and he wanted to tell someone. He needed to talk to Karen.

When he returned home, Karen had already left for work. He thought about whether he could wait for dinner or if he should talk to her sooner? John took a shower and kept wondering what was next. This was the first step in waiting on the Lord, because his calendar was actually blank. There was nothing. He didn't have any interviews or work scheduled. In fact, he hadn't even thought about what he was going to do for the rest of the day.

Usually, John was afraid of idle time. If ever he had free time, he usually worked out or filled that time with something, anything. Everything had a plan, and he would attack it with the determination of someone afraid to stop. It was the first time since he lost his job that he allowed himself to have some downtime. Up until then, he was afraid to be idle.

It hadn't occurred to him until that moment, but he was out of plans. He really had to let go and let God, just like the cliché. What now? He decided to do something that he hadn't done in more years than he could remember. He went to the bookshelf and found the Bible he had since high school. How many times had he moved it to a different home without ever opening it? He may not have been idle over the years, but now as he looked back, his work seemed more like that of a dog chasing his tail in circles: plan, action, motion, activity, sweat, pain—but what was gained?

"Well, Lord, where do I start after all these years?" John asked aloud. He was sitting at his desk looking at his old Bible, trying to remember some of his favorite verses. He felt a kindred connection to Paul out on the trail, so he started to leaf through some of the letters that Paul had written to the Romans, Galatians, and Colossians.

Chapter TWENTY-FOUR

Not long after John began reading his Bible, the phone rang. "Hey John, it's Steve. What's going on?" John hesitated before answering the question. There was so much happening to him now.

"Hey Steve, not much. I'm sitting here trying to decide where to begin a Bible study. What's up with you?"

"That's cool; great way to start your day. Listen, I just got off the phone with Stephanie James from the university. She's interested in talking to you, but she's on the road for the rest of the week and doesn't know if she has a position available. She knows she needs the help and is interested to see if the two of you can work something out. She's a straight-shooter and won't lead you on unless she thinks of some way she can help. So what do you think?"

"Wow, I appreciate your following through. Thanks for making the contact. I'm available whenever. Is there something in particular I should do to prepare for a meeting with her?"

"Well, as a matter of fact, I think some of the research you did on new technologies coming into Michigan would be very interesting to her; especially the stuff you were telling me the other night about your approach for analyzing new business proposals, the kind with very little track record to work off, since she deals primarily with cutting-edge technology not connected to a funding source. I think your approach would be very attractive to her. She's all about getting research into useable, marketable projects. That's her business. She's swamped with ideas but definitely needs help weeding through to see what would be viable and what needs to be tabled. I'd be glad to spend some time with you this week to give you an idea of some of the stuff that I've talked to Stephanie about."

"Steve, that's very generous of you. I'd really appreciate the opportunity to prepare the best I can. This is the kind of thing I dreamed of when I was in school."

"I would like to do this when we have several hours of uninterrupted time. I can't do that during the day this week, though. I'm pretty booked and I have our small group meeting at church tonight. How about coming over tomorrow night so we can go over some of the ideas that are out there?"

"Tomorrow night is great. You know, I woke up this morning with a lot more confidence than my recent adventures would lead me to have. My focus has shifted a bit, too. I know I need to stop thinking about my failures and shortcomings and look at the person I need to be. You said you were pretty busy, but would you be available for lunch today?"

"I do need to eat lunch. I'll be heading out on the road in just a few minutes. I was going to stop for lunch before my next appointment. Can you have an early lunch?"

"Well, my calendar is pretty clear, so sure, anytime works." He chuckled at the idea of juggling his busy calendar.

"What if I stop and pick up some sandwiches and we meet at your house? I have a 1:30 meeting this afternoon on your side of town and that puts me halfway there."

"Great. I'll see you when you get here."

Not long after they hung up, Steve walked in the side door with a bag of sandwiches, as an old friend would, and John called him to come on into the kitchen. They made themselves comfortable at the kitchen table and started to eat. Steve began. "On the phone you mentioned that you were starting a Bible study. What are you studying?"

"I haven't really started studying anything yet. I haven't studied the Bible in several years." John paused and chewed his ham and cheese sandwich for a few moments. "Let's say, I've received some revelations lately that indicate a strong need to get back into the Scriptures. This past month has helped illuminate my life and priorities, and it's kind of pathetic, really. For a guy who's been blessed so much in my life, I guess I've been a dunce when it comes faithfulness and thankfulness. The lessons of childhood—you'd think that I'd at least have remembered those."

"Boy, haven't we all been there, especially people like you and me. We are gifted with pretty strong ambition and good work ethics. We have our plans and we intend to spend our lives putting them in motion. I don't know what you know about me, but I've had this power struggle too. My commitment to the church is not that old. While I was growing up, my family was at church all the time. But for some reason, the message that I needed Christ seemed to allude me. Over the years, my fiercely independent streak has gotten in the way of yielding to Christ. I thought my dad and I were alike, but somehow he was the strong, head-of-the-family guy yet still a humble man in his relationship with the Lord. Once I was out in my law practice and spending time with my parents more as peers than parent-child, I started to notice the differences between my dad and myself."

John sat back in his chair, listening to Steve's story. He was intrigued that two guys from such different backgrounds—one with an intact family, the epitome of the Norman Rockwell painting, and the other raised by a single parent struggling to survive—could need the same thing when they reached adulthood. It wasn't such a mystery, John decided. Humans are human, with the same innate spiritual needs.

John knew he'd made prosperity and security his god. Over the years of striving and sacrificing, he'd decided that all he needed to be satisfied with life was to be successful. That was his goal, after all.

Steve, now finished with his lunch, continued, "I found myself feeling very much alone, despite being with lots of friends, roommates, and family. I felt a void. It was like I was playacting who I wanted to be, or at least who I wanted people to believe I was. I was restless and discontented, even while I was experiencing a lot of apparent success. My busyness distracted me, though, for a long time—too long—so I put it out of my mind and didn't do anything about it."

Steve paused to collect his thoughts before going on. "Last Christmas, I was at a party with some colleagues, and somebody had the gumption to ask about my Christmas plans, not 'holiday plans' as people usually phrase things so as not to offend, but my Christmas plans specifically. That was a bell ringer. Of course, I had a response since I belong to a religious family: I would be going to church. But this person got more specific. He asked if I was doing anything special during the advent season to prepare for Christmas. When I gave him a funny look, he clarified that he didn't mean buying presents and stuff, but rather how was I preparing my heart. This was something I wasn't ready for. I wasn't doing anything special and hadn't thought two seconds about preparing my heart. This is when I started to realize that I was missing something. At the time I shook him off as some religious fanatic, but the question stayed with me.

"I usually spent weekend time with my parents, and at some point or another I noticed that my dad was much more into preparing for Christmas than I remembered. On a Saturday afternoon early in December I asked him if he was more into Christmas now that he had retired and had more time. He laughed and said that he thought it was about the same. But my dad told me how much he loved getting prepared for Christmas, that he felt his spirit come alive when he was serving the Lord. We talked for a long time that day and the following weeks. Through these conversations, I found that, in fact, I was preparing my heart for the coming Christ. Last Christmas was very powerful for me. I finally let down my guard and let Christ in as my Lord, not just as an acquaintance anymore but as the most intimate confidant. My life hasn't been the same since."

John finished his lunch and took a drink of his pop, looked at his new friend, and smiled. "Steve, when I was in high school and a little into college, I was all about asking guys those questions. I went to youth group and was a leader in teen Bible studies. This was important to me. But all the time that I did those things, I prayed that somebody would come forward and make things easier for my mom, you know, a little *quid pro quo*. She worked so hard to give me things she believed I would've had if my dad were alive, things she felt I needed. She was always exhausted, working two and sometimes three jobs so I would be able to go to college. I didn't see answers to these prayers. I didn't get why the Lord wasn't answering. I worried about my mom not having a husband to take care of her when I was gone, but no answer there either.

"In my frustration, I slowly left my Christian activities behind. First, I stopped asking other people about their relationship with Christ and chose not to interfere with their lives. It was none of my business, I decided. Then I became less and less involved with Bible study since I wasn't evangelizing anymore, and I was more comfortable when I wasn't around people who were doing that stuff. I never consciously chose to leave or to renounce my faith. It just faded away until I didn't even recognize it anymore. It was easier to leave it than it was to believe that God didn't care about us. To be honest, until this past month I haven't felt God busting down my door to get me back, either."

Steve shifted in his seat, leaning forward while John spoke. He glanced at his watch to keep track of his time. "I guess everyone has their own story," he said.

John added, "...but the same bottom line! We need a relationship with Jesus. It's not about just knowing He exists. We need to talk to Him; we need to experience Him. That's what I've come to realize. I had a great session with Jeff Martin yesterday."

"Jeff's the reason I'm at this church," Steve chimed in enthusiastically. "I started shopping around to find a church where I could feel comfortable. I needed a place of my own. My parents are such bigwigs in their church, and I didn't want to embarrass them. So I went to the same mega church that Mary attended. Not surprisingly, we never met, even though our time there overlapped.

"The message was presented very effectively, but I'd already spent a great deal of my life just watching the Christian life from the sidelines. It was time I joined the game. So I looked around to find something more intimate, a place I could participate. The other service was more like a presentation. They had small groups for more intimacy, but I wasn't captivated in the service, so I didn't feel compelled to try harder."

"Funny thing, I came to a church service in a gym and found just what I needed, something so worshipful and compelling. I decided to come to this church because of a sign out on the lawn. It's a beautiful building. I never thought I'd be in the gym, but I liked the service and the people from the moment I walked in the door. For the first time, I felt that I was involved in something that was going to move me. It makes a difference to me if I'm there or not. That's what keeps me coming back. Now I've met Mary, and we both feel the same way about the place, so I think this is where I will worship. The hunt is off."

"Are things with you and Mary pretty serious?"

"I think they are. We've only been seeing each other about four or five months, but she seems to be the one. I haven't dated a ton. I have a lot of female friends, but I'm not a shopper. When I met Mary, I knew I wanted to spend more time with her, so I asked her out. I have no desire to see anyone else. We pretty much see each other every day now."

John let the subject drop so as not to pry. He smiled inwardly. He finally had one on Karen. This dude was in love. He was pretty sure that sooner than later, they would be celebrating Steve and Mary's engagement.

Steve rose, "Sorry man, but I have to hit the road. I've enjoyed our conversation. I have to get to an appointment. See you tomorrow night. Why don't you come over at seven o'clock? I'll e-mail you the directions."

Chapter TWENTY-FIVE

OVER THE PAST week John had bided his time waiting for the opportunity to meet with Stephanie James. Now, as everyone else's attention was shifting to Thanksgiving, he was busily preparing for what he hoped was an interview that would change his life. He spoke to Stephanie while she was still on her business trip, and they had good chemistry right off the bat. Arrangements were made to meet the Wednesday before Thanksgiving. The university research departments were involved in some really innovative stuff, and John felt exhilarated reviewing the projects Steve had given him. Stephanie had given Steve permission to share some information to get John's reaction to the scope of the work involved with the projects.

"Hey, honey. How's it going?" Karen asked as she wiped her hands on a towel while walking into the living room. Her assignment for Thanksgiving dinner was to make two pies, and she was done. Now she just wanted to get off her feet and snuggle with her husband on the couch while the pies baked. John was reviewing the financial data he received from Steve and comparing it to the pro forma statements he had put together.

He knew his proposal inside and out. John sat in the middle of the couch, leaning over the pages of work laid before him on the coffee table as he organized his presentation. He was so engrossed, he didn't hear Karen enter the room. She was practically standing on top of him before he noticed she was there.

"Boo!"

"What? Oh, hi. What's up?" John responded, hardly looking up. "I want to be totally prepared for tomorrow morning's interview with Stephanie. I don't even want to look at these pages while I go over the various scenarios to attract investors for this project. You know, I think Steve set me up with a project with some real potential so Stephanie can see what I'm made of. All we hear with the rising gas prices is the need to develop alternative fuels. This project deals with the development of a hydrogen cell that has some real potential."

"Do you want to practice on me? I'd love to hear options you've come up with."

"Sure. I'm just about ready for a run-through. Give me about ten more minutes. OK?"

"I'm going to get into my pajamas while you finish up. I'll put on some decaf coffee for later." Karen went to the bedroom and changed into her comfy, plaid, flannel pajama pants; a red, long-sleeve T-shirt; and her fluffy slippers. She padded back into living room and noticed that John was just about finished as she continued into the kitchen and made the coffee.

"Hey, Karen, are you ready?" John called.

"Yep," Karen returned to the living room with two cups of coffee and a small piece of pecan pie." Handing John his cup, she made herself at home on the wingback chair by the window.

"Only one piece of pie?" John looked both hurt and quizzical.

"I have to taste-test it. You can have some when you're finished. I made an extra pie for us. Now show me what you've got."

For the next forty minutes, John showcased the entire presentation for her. At some point, Karen had put down the plate and had forgotten about the coffee waiting for her. She was mesmerized by the depth of information that John had pulled together in such a short period of time. He'd been working night and day, but Karen had no idea where he came up with this stuff. Stephanie should really be impressed with this work.

"What kind of sources did you use for this information? It sounds really solid."

"Steve gave me the data the researchers submit to their departments, and then I hit the Web to fill in the holes. With the resources available at the university, I could really go to town and come up with some interesting ideas. My problem with this stuff is, it only shows me the potential. I know where I need more facts to beef up the project before it would be anywhere close to a real presentation to prospective investors. But I think, given the limited time and research available, this is pretty good for an interview."

Karen shook her head and took a swig of her coffee. "Who will be at the interview tomorrow?"

"I think it'll be just Stephanie and me. We're meeting at her office in Ann Arbor, so there may be some other people around; but remember, it's the day before a holiday, so my guess is it'll be just us. Can you think of any questions she might ask to practice that part?"

Karen gathered his notes in her hands and asked questions about various aspects of the proposal, about his sources, the timetable of the project and timing of the investment needs, as well as payback periods—the usual financial issues investors like to have spelled out. It was a game they enjoyed playing. It had been a long time since the project was John's and she was the one asking the questions.

"I sense a lot of pent-up creativity coming out here. You enjoyed this more than a little bit," Karen observed. "That'll come out in the interview as well. She's had great references for you from both Steve and Jim Brooks. She approved giving you what I think might be sensitive information. I think you need to go in there and show her what you're made of. You're going to blow her away."

"OK, OK, enough of the pumping up. Help me gather my notes and get them in the proper order. I need a good night sleep, and maybe a little of that pie!"

As they were heading up to bed, John announced, "Hey, honey, I would like to start going to that small group at church. You know, the one that Mary and Steve go to. I hope Steve wouldn't think I was only doing it to get the job. I've talked to him about some of the stuff they've studied and it sounds really interesting. Sometimes they do Bible studies and other times they pick a book to read and discuss. What do you think? Are you interested?"

The question hung out there while John brushed his teeth and got into his pajamas. Karen was sitting up in bed. She thought about the books that Mary brought to work to read at lunch sometimes. While they seemed kind of radical, she was intrigued.

"I think it would be a great idea for a couple of reasons," she stated. "First, we'd meet more people there, which would be a good idea since we both want to get involved. Second, I think they study some stuff that is out-of-the-box kind of thinking. We may not agree with it all, but it might challenge us to think rather than just sit and agree the way we did when we were kids. It could lead to some good discussions. Even some loud ones." She smiled at him mischievously.

"They meet on Tuesday nights; let's start next week. You know, next week starts advent. That would be a terrific time to start a new spiritual group and recommit ourselves to this Christian community."

John turned out the lights feeling positive about the progress he'd made in the last month. He went from the inside of a dirty, stinky Dumpster, down and out without a job, to a new commitment to a church home and a revitalized relationship with Jesus, not to mention the potential of a whole new career.

Karen cuddled up next to John, who no longer tossed and turned all night long, talking in his sleep, and occasionally crying out. She knew the Lord had His hand on the situation. Their prospects just fell together too well to think otherwise. Karen had the next day off and planned to be the June Cleaver model wife and fix John a fabulous breakfast before she sent him off for his interview.

Chapter TWENTY-SIX

THE KITCHEN SMELLED terrific when John returned from his early morning run. Karen turned from the stove as he came through the door. "I was surprised to roll over in bed this morning and find your side empty. What is it out there, 25 degrees?"

"No, it's a little under 40. I was awake early, so I decided that a run would get me going, help me focus, and burn off some nervous energy. I thought about waking you up to come with me," he smiled teasingly at her.

"I made a great breakfast for you: scrambled eggs, turkey sausage, whole wheat toast. I don't want your stomach rumbling during your pitch. Here's your coffee." She handed him his cup and directed him to the table. "It's all ready, so why don't you eat and then shower. I'm kind of hungry; I think I'll join you."

"I didn't know you were going to get up so early," John said, still surprised at the unexpected breakfast. "I appreciate it." As he ate, he realized how important her support was to him. "This tastes perfect. I want to get an early start on the road; the drive to Ann Arbor is about forty-five minutes long, and I have to find the right building and parking. Stephanie's instructions seem pretty clear, but you know how confusing that city can be."

"That's a good idea. Besides, if you get there too early, you can just walk around the campus a bit. Plus, there's that great coffee shop right downtown. You can sit there and review your notes."

John scrapped up the last traces of his breakfast and pushed himself away from the table. After a hot shower and shave, he stood at his closet rethinking the suit-shirt-tie combination he'd picked last night with Karen's input. "No, I'm sticking with last night's choices; her instincts are best," he thought to himself. Dressed in his starched white Polo button-down, his freshly cleaned and pressed navy suit, and the lighter blue tie with the subtle paisley pattern, John thought about the image he was portraying. Was this really him?

One thing his sessions with Jeff and the whole previous month's journey had convinced him of was the absolute need to be honest about who he was and what he was looking for in his life. This, he'd discovered, required an enormous amount of trust. John was so busy being his own man, trusting other people wasn't a skill he had practiced much.

John looked at himself in the mirror. The "Ford uniform," as Karen referred to these highly pressed, highly starched, and highly polished suits of armor, were the clothes he'd gravitated to since college. Moving his shoulders around, he found that he was comfortable. His image in the mirror looked pretty serious, he thought. That much was accurate. Stiff and serious, these were elements of the real John. Not sure if he liked that, but he was who he was.

Someone recently, probably Jeff or maybe Steve, had said that he needed to come to his faith as he was. He didn't need to change himself into anyone else for an authentic relationship with Jesus. Right now, he sure hoped that applied to Stephanie and the job potential at the university! He checked his watch, grabbed his overcoat and briefcase, and headed for the door.

Karen walked up to him, grabbed his waist, and planted a huge kiss on his lips. "Good luck, honey. Have a terrific day!"

The road to Ann Arbor was dry and clear. Traffic was light because of the holiday, and the sun was shining in the rear window and reflecting in the mirrors, giving an ethereal appearance to his car. As he drove, he listened to a Christian music station, something a bit unusual for him. John made good time, and soon he was at the exit for downtown Ann Arbor. He made his way to the parking lot suggested by Stephanie in her e-mail.

His appointment was at nine and the dashboard clock showed that it was just eight-thirty. He pulled up to the gate and opened his window to take the ticket as it popped out of the yellow machine. He easily found a parking spot close to the intersection he needed. It occurred to him that many people took the Wednesday before Thanksgiving off and Stephanie may have come into the office specifically to meet him.

He looked in the rearview mirror and brushed his bangs to the side, but they disobediently fell right back to where they wanted to be. The old desperation was sinking back into his brain as he sat there waiting to go into the office. He closed his eyes and spoke aloud, "Jesus, I want Your plan for me. Things are awfully difficult around here. I need a job, but I want the right one. So if this is it, help me Lord to trust You, trust who You've made me to be. I confess the nervousness and anxiety I'm feeling that is such a part of the old me. Fill me with Your Spirit, Lord. Most of all, Lord," he paused because this was the most important part and the newest to him, "help me be real with Stephanie. I need to show her the real me."

Now it was time. John looked over at his briefcase sitting on the seat beside him, holding his work and preparation for the meeting, hoping against hope that it was sufficient. He took the handle of the case with his right hand and simultaneously opened the car door with his left. He stepped out of his car into the bright sunshine and felt the cool air brush over him. Invigorated, energized, he walked to the stop light on the corner to get his bearings. The street signs said he was at the intersection of Liberty and Second Streets. He looked on a building down on his left and saw the number 309, and John turned and walked toward it. He continued down the block until he reached 345. This was it.

The redbrick building was in the Victorian style but had been revamped to accommodate the needs of the current tenants. It had the mustiness expected in these old buildings with antiquated ventilation. Inside the door, he looked at the registry and found the university enterprise office on the fourth floor. Excitedly, John headed for the stairway. He didn't look for an elevator; there was still a negative feeling in his gut from the last elevator ride he'd taken.

Exiting the stairway at the fourth floor, he didn't have any trouble locating suite 402, and walked to the door. He reached for the handle, drawing forth the much-needed inner confidence. He felt it! There was a surge of hope welling up in him. He wasn't playacting; it was real, like the velveteen rabbit, his favorite story from his childhood. Before him was a bank of four secretary/assistants' work areas, occupied by three women and a man who were busy at their computers. Behind this work area were three offices. The first had a nameplate on the door that read "Stephanie James, Director, Department of Enterprise Services." John walked up to the assistant closest to Stephanie's office, smiled at her, and waited for her to finish her phone call.

After hanging up the phone, the young woman looked up at John, returned his smile, and said, "I'll bet you're John Sheppard."

"Yes, I guess I'm in the right place."

"You guess right. I'm Julie, Stephanie's assistant. Stephanie is expecting you. She's just finishing up a call with the governor's office. She didn't think she would be too long. She asked me to show you around and get you some coffee."

Julie gave a short yet very descriptive tour of the offices. "We've been in this location for about two years now," she explained. "We used to share space with the development office, but we got too big and were kicked out." She chuckled, "They didn't like watching us raise more money for the university than they were." Julie had a good sense of humor. "We're renting this space, but we'll be moving again, since the university doesn't like to pay rent. This works pretty well for us, though, because when we have researchers or investors here for meetings, it's nice to be able to do it 'quietly' if you know what I mean." She made air-quote marks with her fingers as she said the word *quietly*.

John silently took in the tour, intrigued with the set-up of the office. It was different from Ford in that there was some privacy for those who had offices, and the assistants were able to work together on their projects in a spirit of cooperation with plenty of room to spread out their work. The decorating looked like it was recently updated, probably when they moved in. The paint was fresh, the carpet was in good condition, and the furniture was an attractive dark cherry.

Parties entering these offices looking to invest or looking for investors would be impressed with the business atmosphere, categorically nonacademic. There was a positive energy, an atmosphere almost foreign throughout most of Michigan these days. John could hardly put aside the feeling that he would give his right arm to work here. He needed to stop thinking about that, just make his presentation, and leave it there.

Julie and John returned to the conference room, where coffee was waiting. They had just taken their seats when in walked a tall, beautiful African-American woman. She was mesmerizing. Her hair was cut short and she had smooth chocolate skin; huge doe-like brown eyes, and a warm, wonderful smile. Even at six feet tall, she wore heels with her Dolce and Gabbana black corded suit, not afraid to intimidate the timid. Her stride was confident, and when she extended her hand to John, he rose as if on command.

"Hi John, I'm Stephanie James. I've been looking forward to meeting you."

"Hello." John needed to take a deep breath. She was not what he was expecting. There was nothing academic about Stephanie. She had the bearing to match any CEO.

Accustomed to the effect she had on people, Stephanie gave him a few seconds to absorb her presence before speaking. "Both Steve Clark and Jim Brooks have spoken highly of you. I'm excited to see what you think of our little project I sent over."

Julie excused herself by saying, "I have a few things to finish up today. John, it was a pleasure meeting you."

John was still a little flustered, but he managed to shake hands with Julie. "It was my treat. Thanks for the tour." He smiled as she left the room.

Barely able to get his thoughts back in order—it would have been nice if either Steve or Jim had given him a heads-up on this amazing woman—John found he needed to fight off panic. He needed to be professional. These projects, this group of people, were exactly what he dreamed of his whole life. "Don't blow it now," he reminded himself. John had to get it together.

"Well, I wouldn't exactly call a hydrogen cell that can keep a battery charged in an electric car for a full twenty-four hour period—despite being caught in rush hour traffic, traveling across the country on expressways or driving through the mountains—a *little* project," he said, smiling. "Whew, recovered," he sighed to himself. Stephanie smiled back at him. John was reassured.

"Why don't you show me how we can move this from the drawing board to the board room with your feasibility study."

John removed his notes from his briefcase and laid the stack in front of him. He handed Stephanie a set of charts printed in color he'd prepared to accompany his presentation. He sat up in the chair, leaning forward, and began. Once he started, he gave the entire dog and pony show without once looking at his notes, just as he did in his living room the night before. He used the charts to highlight the data he'd gathered. He also pointed out areas he'd like to do more research on before making a pitch to a potential investor.

At the conclusion he asked, "Do you have any questions?"

Stephanie nodded. She'd taken a few notes while John talking. "What were your sources for this data? This is a lot more than I sent to you."

"I went online to research the ins and outs of the hydrogen cell. The idea has been out there for a while, but the practicality has always been in question. I compared this to the information you sent over to see how this project is better than previous attempts in the marketplace. I do have more questions, some things I'd like to clarify with the researchers themselves, but since this is a job interview, I didn't think calling them was appropriate."

"You're a wonderful testimony to our business school. This work is excellent. We need someone who can pick apart these projects so we can spend our time more wisely with really good opportunities. One of my frustrations, one that I have shared with Steve on many occasions, is the amount of time we invest in projects to find that there is already too much competition in the market for them. We can't sell those."

She rose from her seat and walked over to the window. She stood staring out on the city below, hands on both hips. There was a lot of pressure to capitalize on the research the university was producing, however, as usual they were doing so with their hands tied by budget constraints.

"When you arrived I was on the phone with the state's budget director," Stephanie explained. "I told him that in order to get more projects into the market and to keep them in Michigan I need more funding. I bring literally millions of dollars into this university from venture capitalists. It could easily be more. But the money I bring in doesn't stay in my budget. It goes to the university, funds more research, and builds buildings. They don't really get the big picture. A little to play with and they're happy because it's more than they've had in the past. They're used to writing grant requests and relying on those and government handouts. I see this much bigger. I don't want to build buildings; I want to build towns, put people to work. Stop the brain drain from Michigan, make this a mecca of research and development."

This dialogue wasn't going where John wanted. No, she was setting him up for a fall. He could feel it. He could already feel his shoulders drop from the strong, self-assured, position they were in after he'd made his presentation and could tell she liked his work. He knew his face was getting shiny with sweat and his hands were starting to shake. Where was his faith now? Better question, where was God now and that grand plan He had for John's life?

Stephanie hadn't turned around yet. She couldn't face him. "I'm going to be straight with you. I don't have a position available; I don't have the funding because of a hiring freeze at the university. The governor has cut funding to higher education, and that means all of us, apparently. Obviously, I have the work, but I can't get a position approved by the bureaucrats in charge. I feel the desperation you do to keep projects in Michigan; this is my home state. But, unfortunately, my hands are tied. I think you are enormously talented. I'd give my right arm to have you working here with me."

"I appreciate your honesty, Stephanie," John responded. "What do you know about the MEDC and their employee database? Maybe there's some potential for me there."

"Well, I'm sorry to disappoint you, but that's something that hasn't really come to fruition yet. It's still in the talking stages. The Oakland County Executive, L. Brooks Patterson, wants to make it a reality, but he's not getting a lot of help from Lansing, who holds the purse strings of the MEDC."

John had been pinning his hopes on these two options. Now, they had both been shot down. Everything in him wanted to run out of the office and scream. Again, he felt like he had been set up, just to be shot down. God must be having a lot of fun at his expense, he thought. He probably shouldn't have been so dismissive with those headhunters. It didn't look like he was going to get the job of his dreams. Now he just had to get something.

"John, if I come up with anything, you'll be the first I call. I'm sorry I couldn't do better," Stephanie said, clearly sorry.

John stood and shook her hand. Once again he had to drag himself out of an office where he wanted to be. "Thanks for your time. I appreciate the opportunity to show you the kind of work I am capable of. Enjoy your weekend."

Stephanie walked John to the coat closet. He put his coat over his arm and headed out the door. At least there wasn't a security officer making sure he left the premises this time.

Chapter TWENTY-SEVEN

AFTER GOING FOR her own run that morning, Karen decided to surprise John with a very romantic celebration dinner. She went to the butcher at the high-end specialty grocery store and purchased two meaty New York strip steaks. Then she selected two baking potatoes and some large, juicy strawberries, walnuts, mixed greens, and blue cheese for a salad. She picked up a bouquet of roses at the florist and some scented candles for the table.

Back at home, Karen took out the fine china. She still loved the Royal Dalton pattern she'd picked when they were getting married. With the white linen tablecloth she'd inherited from her grandmother; the silverware, all polished and ready for the holidays; flowers; and candles, the table was complete and beautiful.

In the kitchen, the steaks were seasoned and waiting. The potatoes were poked and wrapped in foil, and the salad was ready to go. The rest of the time she could prepare herself with a nice, long, hot scented bath. One major benefit of their house was a Jacuzzi whirlpool tub in the master bath that had been installed by a previous owner. Karen didn't take advantage of it very often, but today was the perfect opportunity.

She was a little surprised John wasn't home yet. "This must be good," she thought. If the job worked out, they might have a lot of details to work through. Karen stepped into the tub feeling confident.

John walked around downtown Ann Arbor. The streets were deserted since most of the students had already left for the long holiday weekend. The wind was blowing the leaves and some debris along the sides of the buildings and curbs. The sky was gray, and John found himself once again in a desolate mood. How had he allowed himself to get so excited for this job opportunity with all he'd gone through this past month? When was he going to learn that he couldn't count on good things happening? They just didn't happen to him. It was ridiculous. As the afternoon wore on, John found himself getting angrier and angrier.

The question was, though, who was he angry at? Himself? Stephanie James for setting him up for such a disappointment? Steve, for sticking his nose in where it didn't belong? God? Well, definitely God. The Almighty certainly had it in His power to keep this from happening, in so many ways. John's temper was rising. This walk wasn't doing him any good. He figured he may as well just head home.

John got back to his car and he made his way to the expressway. There were no police around, and John floored it all the way across M–14 and back to Birmingham, his temper raging all the way. He pulled into the garage and slammed his car door. Still not feeling any better, he slammed the door to the house as well. Karen was standing in the kitchen in a sexy black cocktail dress. He brushed past her, not even giving her a second look. He pounced his way through the house and up to the bedroom, where he slammed that door as well.

Karen got the message. It didn't go well, not at all. She stood in the kitchen utterly speechless.

Chapter TWENTY-EIGHT

THE WEEKEND WAS miserable. Together with Sharon, Karen convinced John to join them at her parents' house for the annual Thanksgiving get-together. Karen's entire family was present: all three of her sisters with their husbands; her two little nieces, who belonged to her middle sister; as well as her mother and stepfather. Everyone knew what John had faced this past month. They would be a friendly, easygoing crowd. John agreed to go, but he didn't agree to be happy.

Everyone felt the tension. John sat there sulking, chin pressed into his chest, shoulders slouched, slunk down in his chair while he graced them with his presence at the table. Conversation went on around him, but he remained estranged from the group. He didn't even take part in watching the football game. Karen couldn't help but feel perturbed, and approached him about it. "I know you're angry, but you don't have to ruin everyone's day."

John shot back, his eyes glaring, "I didn't want to come. You are the one who forced the issue. You should have just left me alone."

Karen knew he was right, she felt between a rock and a hard place. "All right, let's go home and end this madness."

John, Karen, and Sharon were the first to leave, much to the relief of everyone else. Karen kissed her parents and hugged her little nieces goodbye. She apologized for ruining the day.

Speaking for the group, Jane said, "Oh, honey, we understand. We hate to see you so worried. Just keep believing; something will turn up soon."

Karen just shrugged. She wondered what would turn up. Her faith was not as shaken as John's. She wasn't sure why. But, she did believe that this was still an important part of the plan. She was all about plans.

Karen had shared her new faith with her mother. Jane had come to know the Lord when her first marriage broke up and prayed with Sharon many times for the return of their children to the Lord. When Jane said to "just keep believing," she meant keep believing in the Lord. Karen knew her mother worried that since her faith was so new, she might turn away from Jesus again. This was not going to happen. Karen had to help John see that his faith was just as real now as it was yesterday morning before the interview.

The threesome got into the Escape, and with Karen at the wheel, waved good-bye and drove back to Sharon's. She worked to break the silence, "Mom, do you want to go shopping with us tomorrow?"

"Sure, I'd like that. Who's going?"

"Just the girls, big girls that is; my mother and sisters. No babies."

"That sounds like fun. I assume there's a lunch involved with this outing."

"Absolutely, my sisters aren't going to head back to the roost one minute before they have to. Besides, there's always so much football on, the guys won't even miss them." She looked over at John in his angry stupor and amended her statement, "None of us will be missed."

They pulled up in front of Sharon's house. "See you tomorrow. What time are we getting together?"

"I'll pick you up at nine o'clock. That way we'll get a nice, early start. See you then." She gave Sharon an appreciative smile and looked at John, who didn't even register that his mother left the car. "Whew, this is not fun," Karen thought to herself.

At home, John went right up to bed. It was still early and Karen looked around trying to decide what to do. She thought about calling Mary, but she and Steve had gone to her family's house for Thanksgiving and wouldn't be back until Sunday. They'd left on Wednesday and John probably hadn't contacted Steve to let him know what happened at the meeting.

Karen didn't want to go upstairs since John was there and had made it pretty clear he wanted to be alone. John had his back to the wall without options, again. This was not a place he did well. His brooding had reached a toxic level. The only one who had any chance of getting through to John now was the Lord. Karen decided she was going to trust Him.

She sat on the couch and opened her new Bible. At the back of the Bible was a concordance. Since she didn't know the Book very well, she went there and started to look up verses that might help. First, she looked up the word *trust*. "'Trust in God' has four verses. Let's see what Psalm 20:7–9 has to say. 'Some trust in chariots, and some in horses, But we will remember the name of the Lord our God. They have bowed down and fallen, But we have risen and stand upright. Save, Lord! May the King answer us when we call.'"

Karen was amazed that the Bible was so easy to use. "Wow, that's what I needed to hear. We must be careful what we trust in. Trust in the wrong things, earthly things, that leads to defeat. Even a king needs to trust in the Lord in order to know victory." Karen was talking out loud, even though she was alone in the living room.

"Lord, help me to keep my eye on You, to trust You. Help me to encourage John to do the same. I know You are hurting with him. This must be part of the plan; we must have more we are to learn from this situation. Help us to have eyes to see and ears to hear." Karen closed the Bible and sat, meditating on the Scripture she was given, receiving the encouragement she needed.

Monday morning finally dawned. Karen rose and spent some time reading the Bible. Now that she found the concordance, she was finding meaning in Scripture all over the place. She was even getting pretty quick at finding the books in the Bible. She couldn't wait to tell Mary how much she'd learned over the weekend. She would also have to tell her about John's disappointment of not getting the job. Karen showered, dressed, and headed off to work before John even considered getting up. He'd spent most of the weekend sleeping. It was hard to believe that he could stay in bed too much longer.

At 9:30, John was still lying in bed, awake and staring at the ceiling when the phone rang. He considered not answering; it was probably his mother checking in on him. At the fourth ring, he picked up the receiver without looking at caller ID.

"Hello."

"Hello, John? This is Stephanie James."

John bolted upright in bed. "Hi Stephanie. What can I do for you?"

"John, I've spent a lot of time over the weekend trying to work out a way we can use your services here at the university. I've spoken to the provost and the state budget director. I really need your services. The way you analyzed the project I sent over was amazing. I think you would most likely save us a ton of money and time and help us keep these projects right here in Michigan."

This was sounding good. Maybe they found some money. Maybe something good would happen after all.

"What I'd like to do is hire you as a consultant, on a project-by-project basis," she proposed. "What do you think? You form your own consulting company, and I hire you to do this work. It's a win-win."

"What?" John thought, almost frantic. "This isn't a job offer, not one with security, at least. This is nothing. The university gets what they want, but where does that leave me."

He replied, "Boy, I'll have to think about this. I've never considered going out on my own before. Can I get back with you?"

"Sure, John. I know this isn't your first choice, but right now and until September, this is the best I can do. You did a great job selling me on your skills; you showed a lot of hope for people to venture out on their own with new products and services. This is merely an extension of that thought process, but working for yourself. There's more cash involved for consultants, just no benefits or long-term commitment. With your skills, I wouldn't worry about a long-term need, and you said your wife's job is providing your health insurance. Think about it, John. I really believe this is a great plan for you."

"Thanks, Stephanie. I do appreciate you going out on the limb for me. I need to consider my options. I'll call you back within a couple of days."

"I'm looking forward to hearing from you and working with you. Until then, good-bye."

As John said good-bye and hung up, he felt the bile rise in his throat. "This is not what I prayed for," he said out loud. "This is not a win-win. I will be more like a part-time employee, who's not even an employee. What does that get me?" He continued to sulk.

Chapter TWENTY-NINE

JOHN WAS DOWN in the kitchen in his running clothes, stomping around, pouring coffee, and reheating it. He leaned against the counter stewing. He was still angry, but without other options. No one else was banging down his door to hire him. He started to gag, and suddenly his coffee cup dropped to the floor, breaking into a million glass shards and spilling coffee all over the place. He dropped to his hands and knees, clawing at his face and throat, trying desperately to get rid of the smell. It wouldn't go away. The Dumpster stench was back and with a vengeance.

John reeled and screamed, "Lord, I can't stand this. Help me! I'm losing my mind." He cried and begged for relief, but the stench got stronger and stronger. His hands were being cut by the pieces of glass. He didn't notice. He couldn't get his breath. "Please God, take me now. I can't breathe."

He collapsed on the floor, on top of the glass, in the puddle of coffee. He whimpered, rubbing his face with his bloody hands, begging. This is what he was reduced to.

"Oh God, this isn't my fault. I've always tried to do everything right my whole life. What has it gotten me? Sure, I haven't always been faithful, and I haven't always been spiritual. But changing my ways hasn't served me very well, either. I went back to church, prayed, studied the Bible—all the things that define a 'good Christian.' False hopes, that's all I've got to show for it, for my life. Can you pay bills with false hopes? No! Can you take care of your mother with false hopes? No! I need a job I can count on, one with security, with a pension plan for the future. This consulting thing is bogus, just hype to get my work for nothing. No way! I deserve better than this. My mother deserves better than this. She never turned her back on the Lord. No, she serves Him faithfully day and night. What does she have to show for it? I can't even take care of her. Bah!"

The phone rang. "God, who's it this time," John sighed, exasperated. "Somebody wanting to sell me a cemetery plot? Go away," he shouted at the phone. It kept ringing. "Why doesn't it go to voicemail? It's been ringing forever." It kept ringing and ringing. It wouldn't stop. "Somebody is very persistent. Who could it be?" John was bewildered. It was strange; it should have gone to voicemail.

"Hello?" John asked tentatively, almost expecting God to be on the other end of the line.

"Hey, bro, what's up? I thought we were getting together this morning. How did the interview go?"

It was Jeff. "Well, it's not God Himself," John thought, "but Jeff was a direct link to Him. No wonder he was exempt from voicemail."

"Hey, I forgot," he told Jeff. "The interview went great, all except for the part of not getting the job. Not hiring. Nothing they can do about it. Willing to accept my services as a consultant." John spoke in fragments, out of energy, out of hope.

"Wow, man. I'm sorry. I know you were really counting on this. But, what do you mean by 'consultant.' I'm just a poor preacher; I don't understand."

"Well, if I set up my own company, they will hire me on a project-by-project basis. In other words, no security."

"Oh, I get it." Jeff knew John well. He knew how important security was to him. "Would it be all right if I came over so we could talk?"

"Yeah, whatever. Come on over."

"Great," Jeff tried hard to express encouragement. "I'll be there in about a half hour. Are you guys in the book?"

"Yeah?"

"OK. See you soon."

After hanging up, John looked at the mess. Glass and coffee were all over the kitchen, and his clothes, hands, and face were covered with blood. "This does not look good. Who cares?" He continued to sit in the kitchen on the edge of a kitchen chair, thinking about cleaning up but lacking energy to do it.

The doorbell rang. Without waiting for an answer, Jeff opened the door and stuck his head in. "Hello, John. It's me, Jeff. Can I come in?"

John walked through the living room and into the foyer. "Sure, come on in." He hadn't cleaned up anything. He still looked pretty bad.

"Wow, man. Have you been attacked?"

"Yeah, the Dumpster smell came back after Stephanie's call. I haven't been able to get rid of it. Can't you smell it? It hasn't gone away. I'm almost used to it. I think I'll be smelling this for the rest of my life. I guess this is how homeless people are. They just get used to it."

Jeff was worried. He hadn't seen anything like this before. He knew John was suffering. "Why don't we sit down and talk," Jeff said as he steered John over to the sofa, his hand gently pressing into his back. He didn't want to hurt him since he still had glass all over him.

"You've had these panic attacks with the Dumpster smell a few times, right?"

"Yeah."

"Did you have anything like them before you lost your job at Ford?"

"No, never."

"Well, that's good. I think they're God's way of getting your attention, then. What do you think He's trying to tell you?"

"Honestly, I don't know."

The phone rang again. John gave it a cold glare. "I'm not answering it," John said.

Jeff looked at the caller ID, "It's Steve. Do you mind if I answer? I called and left a message with him that I was coming over here."

"Whatever. Go ahead."

"Hi Steve, it's Jeff. I'm here with John, and he's in pretty rough shape. Can you come over?"

John started waving and mouthing, "No! I don't want to see him."

Jeff ignored him, "Great, we'll see you in a few minutes."

"Jeff, I said I didn't want to see him. I don't want him to see me like this."

"Why don't you go upstairs and shower? I'll clean up the mess down here."

John walked up the stairs, dragging, no energy, no resolve.

Jeff headed in the kitchen and cleaned up the broken cup, the spilled coffee, and the blood.

The doorbell rang, and Steve walked in. Jeff met him in the living room. John hadn't come back downstairs yet. "He didn't get the job he wanted at the university. They offered him an opportunity to be an independent consultant, but the lack of security sent him into a tailspin. He had another panic attack with the Dumpster odor. I think that God's trying to get his attention, trying to point out that his security needs to come from the Lord, not his employer."

"He's had a couple of these attacks before, hasn't he?"

"Yes, but they started when his security had been taken from him. Help me help him, would you?"

"Sure, anything. He's a great guy, talented, insightful, and obviously spiritually sensitive to suffer so."

Jeff smiled. He was right to call Steve. They saw the same thing in John.

John came down the stairs in jeans and a crewneck sweater. He'd showered, his hands covered with the cuts from the glass had stopped bleeding.

"Feel better?"

"Yeah, sure."

"Why don't we sit here in the living room and talk about your anxieties. You do the talking; we'll just listen and maybe ask a few questions. Is that all right?" Jeff knew what he was doing. His counseling skills were sensitive and insightful. He let the Lord do the work. He was merely the conduit.

John was hesitant to start, but he did have a lot on his mind. "I grew up without knowing my dad. My whole life I have striven for one thing, a job—security for my family, the future, and me. It's the one thing I need. When I lost my job at Ford, it was the first time since I was fourteen I didn't have a job. They stripped me of my security. I haven't dealt with that well. I thought that if I turned my life over to the Lord, my need for security would go away. It didn't. The first real test was this position at the university, and when I didn't get it, I went back into the tailspin.

"Surprisingly though, I was just mad. I didn't have the panic attack until Stephanie called this morning and offered me the opportunity to work as a consultant. The idea of work without the security of an employer was the tipping point. It was the same feeling I had when the garbage truck was emptying the Dumpster. I couldn't stop myself from following the other trash into the belly of the garbage truck. I felt myself slipping, sliding along the greased decline into the abyss. It's not the work I'm afraid of. It's not having an employer, someone I can count on to take care of me, so I can take care of my family."

Steve asked, "Do you mind if I ask you a question?"

John nodded to go ahead.

"When you think about an employer, do you always think about a paternal figure, someone taking care of you?"

"I used to. Since Ford let me go, I've had some difficulty with that picture. Hence my anxiety."

"This security thing, it sounds like a synonym for *foundation*. What do you think?"

"Yeah, that's not too much of a stretch. Security, securing to a foundation," John said. He looked over at Jeff, remembering one of their sessions. "I'm thinking that if I'm not supposed to build my house on the sand, and that sand represents my wife and mother, they probably shouldn't build their houses on the sand either, if that sand represents me. We all need a foundation much more secure. If that foundation is God for each of us, then it can't be an employer."

Jeff and Steve both let out a giant "whoop!" and Jeff said, "I think he's got it."

John was up and walking around the room, "Let's think about this. My earthly father couldn't be around to raise me—not his choice, just a bad break. My employer out of college couldn't keep me on, apparently—not their choice, just a bad break. The employer of my dreams can't hire me—not their choice, just bad budgeting. All these earthly sources of security have fallen short of my needs, none of them by choice. So, they would be bad sources of security. But I've been rejecting my heavenly Father, who knows my needs, every hair on my head, and cares for me and loves me as His own, as my source of security. Doesn't sound too smart."

Jeff came to his defense. "Well, trusting in the unseen over the seen is a pretty big step. Faith is not for the weak. It takes a daily walk with the Lord in order to recognize His handiwork. This builds trust. If it were easy, everyone would do it."

"Well, I'm officially out of options, so I guess letting go and letting God is my only choice. I need a better foundation than I've experienced. These storms of life are too hard to brace on my own."

"Amen, brother. It's too hard for any of us. That's the truth of it."

"So what would be a good name for my new consulting business? Something that would be a testament of getting me where I need to be."

Chapter **THIRTY**

I'M READY TO call the university, but first there is an important call to make," John told his visitors. John picked up his cell and called Karen at work.

"Hi, honey. Is everything all right?"

"Well, I don't really know how to answer that question, but I have been doing some serious soul searching with the help of both Jeff and Steve. What would you think about my starting my own consulting business?"

"John, wow, that's an abrupt change. What brought this on?"

"First, Stephanie called this morning and can hire me as a consultant, even though she can't hire me as an employee. She has offered me work."

"Oh, man. That's great. Would it be projects like the one you worked on last week for your interview?"

"Yes, and more. She says that she has a lot of projects that need to be analyzed. It sounded almost like a full-time job."

"Honey, it's what you were made to do. I can't imagine why you would consider saying anything but yes to such a proposal."

"You sound like you feel pretty strong about it."

"Definitely. When can you start? How about that?"

"OK, then. I'll call Stephanie. Talk to you tonight."

"Actually, I'm on my way home. I'll be there in a few minutes."

"Thanks for your support, honey. I'll see you in a few."

With both Jeff and Steve standing at his side, John called Stephanie James back. "Hi, Stephanie, this is John Sheppard."

"Hi John, I didn't think I'd hear from you so soon. I hope you have good news for me."

"Well, I hope you consider it good news. I've decided to step out on faith and start my own consulting company. I'd like to get together to get a better picture of what your expectations will be so I know what I need to organize."

"John, I'm so excited. Let's get together this week. I have a lot of projects coming down the pike and I am really interested in hearing your complete analysis of the hydrogen cell project you've already started on. When you come, I need a bid from you with your rates so that I can get you into the system."

"That sounds great. It will take me a couple of days to get a bid together, especially since I hadn't considered this option until this morning. I want the bid to be well thought out."

"I expect nothing less from you. Do you think we could meet on Thursday or Friday?"

"Let's make it Thursday. That way if I need to do some follow-up, I can get to it on Friday before the weekend."

"Great, let's have a celebratory lunch at Barton Hills Country Club at noon, my treat."

"Stephanie, thanks for your support," John said sincerely. "I'm looking forward to lunch and a long association with you."

John hung up the phone and turned to Jeff and Steve. "Well gentlemen, it's done," he said. "I'm officially self-employed. We're meeting for a celebration lunch on Thursday."

There were high fives all around. They were laughing and slapping one another on the back. Steve chimed in, "I'm looking forward to working with you. My work is almost exclusively through the university. They have so much research going on and so many researchers who want to get in on the resurrection of Michigan, they pretty much keep me busy full time."

"Are you guys available for dinner tonight?" John asked. "I'd like to treat you and your wife and girlfriend to dinner to celebrate. I'd never have been able to do this, understood this, without your guidance."

"Well, I wasn't supposed to tell you. But celebrating is not exclusive to you. I proposed to Mary this weekend. While we were at her parents' house, I asked her dad for her hand in marriage. Once he gave his consent, I couldn't wait for Christmas. I had the ring with me. And, she said yes."

Once again, there were high fives all around. John gave his buddy a great big hug, "Congrats, man. Couldn't happen to a nicer guy."

"But there's more," Jeff added. They both looked at him, faces blank.

"You're already married and you have a great job. Well, maybe it doesn't pay great, but we love it. What's up?"

"Well, Bridget and I are going to be adding to our nest," Jeff explained. "We're having another baby."

"Oh, man! How far will they be apart?"

"A little under two years. For late starters, we're going like gangbusters now."

"OK, everyone must celebrate," John said. "Check with your respective families and see if we can make a seven o'clock reservation at Northern Lakes Seafood. That's a great place to celebrate—everything."

Karen walked in from work finding a houseful of jubilant men. First, she looked at Steve and said, "I know what you're so excited about." She gave Steve a huge, "welcome to the family" hug.

They all laughed. John walked over to his wife and gave her a huge kiss. "Why don't we all go out tonight and celebrate?"

"Your husband already invited us," Jeff explained, "and we're going to try to meet at seven. I better get a hold of Bridget. One of us needs to find a sitter for the little man. I better go. You look like you're in good company, bro. See you tonight."

Steve had his cell phone out and was calling Mary while the others were bringing Karen up to speed. "Hey, honey, are you available for a celebration dinner tonight at seven with the Sheppards and the Martins? Great. I'll meet you at your house in ten minutes. I love you, too."

Both Karen and John had stopped what they were doing and smiled at Steve from ear to ear. They couldn't be happier for Mary or Steve. They were perfect for each other.

Steve looked back at the Sheppards. He, too, was grinning from ear to ear. "OK, we'll see you at the restaurant. Later." He was out the door.

John spent the next two days collaborating with Steve and talking to financial consultants already in the field, connections from Jim Brooks. He wanted to understand the details of establishing his own firm, as well as the ins and outs of the consulting business. People were helpful. He was referred to a professional association he could join to build collegial relationships and participate in continuing education. The association would also increase his creditability when approaching clients other than the university and give him access to business information he'd need as a private business owner. John was excited. This was really going to happen.

On Thursday morning he sat at the kitchen table with his proposal to the university printed on handsome new stationary with his new firm's name at the top: Sheppard Financial Consulting Services, LLC. He sat and stared at it. This was something the old John could not have pulled off. Now he was a new creature in Christ, and he was beginning to see the ramifications of making such a commitment.

Karen walked up behind him and gave his shoulder a squeeze. She reached around him and set a small, gift-wrapped box on top of the papers in front of him. "What's this?" He raised his heavy eyebrows at her in surprise.

"Open it and see."

John picked up the box and shook it. Nothing rattled or ticked. "Guess it's not a bomb," he joked.

"No, guess not." Karen remained nonchalant, poured herself a cup of coffee, turned around, and leaned against the counter while she waited patiently for John to open the present.

Finally, after thoroughly analyzing the exterior of the box, John unwrapped the package. He lifted the top of the box, and there in front of him was a beautiful leather business card case engraved with his initials. He picked it up and rubbed the leather between his fingers. It was smooth, finely finished, expensive dark brown leather. He opened the case, and there were his new business cards. His first business cards ever. This was not something that Ford wasted money on, not for mere contract negotiating analysts. John smiled at Karen. She really believed in him.

The lunch with Stephanie went smoothly. She didn't balk at the professional rate of $125 per hour plus expenses. Apparently she had done her homework as well and knew what to expect. John could have charged much more. He would be one of the cheapest expenses involved in bringing some of the projects to the marketplace. One of the realities that came out of the lunch was the sheer volume and timetables involved with these projects. Steve hadn't been joking when he described her need to hire some help.

Other consultants talked to him about the dangers of setting up his entire business around one client. With the workload, John didn't see how he would have any time to cultivate opportunities with other clients, but this was a start. He was excited.

On the drive home, John got an idea, something kind of outrageous. He would need to talk to Karen about it that night. They sat in the living room that evening with a fire in the fireplace and some soft jazz music playing softly in the background, reflecting on their reversal of fortune. John gave Karen the play-by-play of the meeting with Stephanie. She was looking forward to meeting Stephanie herself. She wanted to express her gratitude for the confidence she showed in John.

"As I drove back from Ann Arbor today I had a revelation," John began.

"Tell me about it."

"What would you think about bringing other people into the consulting business? There is a lot of work to be done. I think it will pay well. And, well, the work is complicated, and some of my best stuff comes when I bounce ideas off other people. I was thinking of calling my old boss, Alan, to see if he might be willing to join me in the business. What do you think?"

"Would you be obligating yourself to a salary? Benefits? I don't think you're ready for that. You haven't even started with your first client yet."

"Yeah, I know it's kind of out there. But I think I'm supposed to share this turn of events. I know it sounds soon, but I think I need to have a partner. I don't feel like the loner I used be, like I have to do everything myself. I have close male friends for the first time in my adult life. This has been one of the greatest gifts of this whole episode. I've always respected Alan. When I wrote up my proposal, I didn't say that I would be doing all the work. I think they would pay for consulting time from any analyst I had working with me, but I would have to approve the work. I would be responsible for the standard."

"I have enjoyed watching you get to know Steve and Jeff," Karen shared. "These are important relationships for you. Friendship is not a little thing; fellowship with other believers is an important part of the Christian experience. Do you know where Alan stands with his faith?"

"No, we never talked about it. It wasn't important to me when we worked together, so I wouldn't know about how he feels about spiritual matters. But, Karen, when I needed help, Steve didn't say, 'Become a Christian first and then I can help you.' He extended his hand to help. The rest was up to the Lord. He was willing to talk, but it was never a deal breaker."

"I guess you're right. You always said Alan was smart. Why are you focusing on him, rather than on someone your own age or with similar experience? He's a little older than you."

"I'm not sure why him and not someone else, but his name came to mind immediately when I got this idea. He doesn't threaten me. I think I'd like working with him, and the two of us together would produce the best work. That's the bottom line. I don't know if he's available. He might have already gotten another position. Well, what do you think? Should I call him?"

"John, why don't we pray about this?" Karen took his hands in hers and they bowed their heads together, seeking God's will in their life and in the life of this new venture. "Lord, we have committed ourselves to You," she prayed. "We desire Your will for our lives. Lead us, Lord. Show us how you want us to proceed and who you want us to reach out to. We thank You for Your love and this opportunity to serve You." She went on affirming their love for Jesus and for one another and expressed their awe at how God alone had turned their lives around. "In Jesus' name we pray. Amen."

John looked up Alan Turner on the Internet and found his contact information. John jotted down the information and picked up the phone. He was certain that this was the right move. He knew that this was what God wanted him to do.

"Hello."

"Hi, Alan. This is John Sheppard; I worked with you at Ford."

"Oh, hi John," Alan responded, surprised and curious. Why was this guy calling, he wondered. After all, he had let him go. He hoped John wasn't going to get on his case or anything. Alan didn't have the strength for that. Although apprehensive, he asked, "What can I do for you, John?"

"Well, I want to talk to you about a business opportunity. I've made some connections with the University of Michigan, and I think I'm going to need some help."

Alan's brain tried processing John's lead. This was not one of those multilevel sales schemes but a position with real promise working with the university. He wondered, what kind of connection could John have with Michigan? "Oh, that's interesting," Alan replied. "What kind of help?"

"Alan, have you found a new position yet?"

"No, nothing. I have six months' severance, like you. But I'm beginning to think that if I'm going to get a new job, it's going to have to be outside of Michigan."

"Well, unless you really want to move out of state, I don't think that's going to be necessary. Can we get together to talk? I'd like to bring you in on this work for the university."

"Yeah, sure. Why? I mean, when?"

"How about tomorrow? I need to get to work on Monday on a new project. This is a beginning, but I think this could be exciting. We might just get to keep a couple of smart guys here in Michigan. Let's meet at the Starbucks at Maple and Lahser and see if this is something you're interested in. How about nine-thirty?"

"Sure, I'll be there. See you tomorrow."

John turned back to Karen and smiled. "We're on our way."

"OK, buddy, now you have to feed me. I'm starved."

John was waiting at the table when Alan walked in dressed casually in khakis and a sweater, not exactly job interview attire. John wore a suit, ready for serious business. John felt more comfortable doing business when he was dressed for business. Maybe he should have joined the FBI, as Mary often teased. John had several folders in front of him with tabs indicating proposed consulting contractor agreements; a description of Sheppard Financial Consulting (SFC), including a mission statement; and one for proposed projects with the University of Michigan, a client to SFC. John tried to think of everything.

When Alan approached, he was a little stunned. "You don't look like you've suffered much by losing your job at Ford."

John looked at him with a wry smile. "If you only knew," he replied dryly. "But I've moved on. Have a seat. I'll show you what I have in mind." John talked about his acquaintance with Stephanie James and her encouragement to establish his own firm to get around the hiring freeze at the university. He described the university's enterprise services department and their potential to rekindle the Michigan economy. The key was to keep projects in Michigan to protect jobs and basically bring money into the state.

John spoke with passion. His hands moved over the papers pointing out different attributes of the documents as he went from one file to another. He explained his vision for the firm and how he saw it serving the community. His excitement was contagious.

Alan watched him with growing interest. Clearly, he'd been skeptical at the outset about the meeting and the opportunity John wanted to show him. He was sure this was going to be some kind of pyramid scheme. When John was assigned to his department at Ford after completing his graduate degree, Alan was leery. He'd thought of John as kind of a corporate pawn, a corporate ladder-climbing competitor. Through the year they had worked together, John had supported him completely and done a great job, often making Alan look pretty good with the higher-ups. John's patience with the corporate system was both helpful to Alan in managing the department and unusual of someone with such talent. John wasn't a boat rocker; he bided his time.

As the presentation drew on, Alan found himself becoming more interested in the project. He saw real possibility. He asked questions. It would definitely be a risk to abort his national job search and choose to stay in Michigan to work with John. But the idea was so compelling, Alan found himself thinking more in those terms than of leaving the state. There would be no benefits, no retirement package—things he'd become used to—but neither would there be the corporate mentality, Big Brother watching, and yes, taking care, of you. Being a pioneer was a change in paradigm. Could he get his head around that? It was something to consider.

"John, I think you're on to something here," Alan said. "I'm used to the security of corporate America, and frankly, at my age, I'm not sure I can change those expectations. I need some time to think about this."

"Absolutely. When I thought about a need to bring in someone to work with me, I thought of you. I appreciated the way you took me into your department back at Ford and tried to give me the highest quality of assignments. I think we bring different skills to the table and would be a strong team. I'm starting the work on Monday with an appointment with the researchers on a project I used for my interview. It would be good to have you there if you want to work with me. That way you'll get up to speed sooner. We understand each other and we both can excel in this business."

"John, I appreciate your high opinion of me. I'm definitely intrigued. I'll get back to you soon, one way or another." He stood and shook John's hand. As he walked to the door, he looked back over his shoulder, smiled at John, and nodded his head, amazed. This was most certainly more than he'd anticipated.

John wasn't worried. He knew this was divine inspiration, and whether Alan accepted his offer or not, he had to put it out there. The rest was between Alan and God. He would push ahead with his new life. This attitude of not worrying was liberating. Why hadn't he tried it earlier in his life? This, he could get used to.

There was still one more person John felt compelled to contact: Liz Sheridan, one of the assistants from his former employer. "If she's still available, it would be very helpful to have her on board for significant number crunching and database building," he thought. He knew he couldn't afford to hire her outright, but if he could get her to do some freelance work, it could help pay her bills and he would be so much more effective. John went online while still at Starbucks and looked up Liz's phone number.

Liz was home when the phone rang. The phone had been deathly silent since she lost her job last month. When she couldn't afford to go out with her friends, they stopped calling. It was like being laid off was contagious, and they sure didn't want to catch it. When the phone rang, she was almost stunned. "Hello?"

"Hi, Liz? This is John Sheppard from your Ford days."

"That explains the call," she thought. "Since he's already laid off, he can't catch the disease. He probably wants to gloat about his new job. He was such a go-getter while at Ford."

Interrupting her train of thought, she responded, "Hi, John. What can I do for you?"

"Liz, how have your job prospects gone? Have you lined up another job?"

"No. How about you?"

"Well, I've decided to go out on my own, start a new consulting business. I've already lined up my first client, the University of Michigan. I was wondering if you might have some time to work with me on a *per diem* basis. I can't afford a regular employee yet, but I need to get started and I need the help."

"Are you kidding? I really need a full-time job since I'll lose my COBRA benefits at the end of eighteen months, but right now I really could use the cash. I didn't get any severance money. I'm broke."

"Cash I can pay. Hopefully before eighteen months is up, I'll be able to afford to pay benefits. But I can't promise that now. I just have to step out on faith. What do you think?"

"How soon can I start? How does that sound?"

"How about Monday? I'm at my new temporary office, the Starbucks at Maple and Lahser in Birmingham. Can you meet me here?"

"You bet. I live about twenty minutes away. I'll see you soon."

John couldn't believe what he'd done and the peace he felt. He, John Sheppard, had actually struck out on his own. He was his own boss. Instead of sitting at home and waiting for the phone to ring, he was making calls and, hopefully, changing people's lives. In yielding his life to Christ, he'd gained autonomy. What a strange paradox.

He was going to need a lot of help to make this come to fruition. It was strange. His new life was scary and exhilarating at the same time. He needed to be sure he was constantly relying on the Lord as his source of wisdom and strength. He wasn't going to walk away from that source again. There would be no more going it alone. The next time the storms hit, and he was certain they would, he would have a foundation he could depend on.

As John waited for Liz to arrive, he took a few minutes to look around the coffee shop. He appreciated the change in his circumstances. If he wasn't sure who he was, at least he knew whose he was. And that was a huge change.

The economic situation in this community was difficult, and it played itself out on the faces of the many people coming and going. He looked at their faces. Each had a story to tell. Some seemed to be meeting friends, waiting to hear the latest gossip, while others were looking around, hoping they wouldn't be sitting alone too long. Many had worried looks on their faces, bedraggled, as though their life situation was taking its toll and they needed the caffeine to keep them going. There seemed to be job interviews happening in one corner, maybe for an opportunity to work at Starbucks, maybe for somewhere else. There was a relief in knowing that he was the one doing the interviewing this time instead of the other way around.

John refilled his coffee and wrote down some notes to go over with Liz. After all, he had a future to prepare.

To Contact the Author

Jill Wilkinson

P.O. Box 2531

Birmingham, MI 48012-2531

Jill629@aol.com

www.wilkinsoncreations.com